RIVER OF DIAMONDS

DROWNED EARTH

DROWNED EARTH

Eight novellas.
Eight Australian authors.
One watery apocalypse.

Scientists said that it would take 5000 years for Earth's oceans to rise.

They were wrong.

After an asteroid collides with Antarctica, a tsunami devastates the world's coastal cities and escalates the melting of the ice caps.

These eight novellas set in various locations around Australia explore the potential consequences of such a catastrophe. They can be read in any order.

Prequel short story: Shards of Silver by Alanah Andrews
The Rise by Sue-Ellen Pashley
Fire Over Troubled Water by Nick Marone
Submerged City by Austin P. Sheehan
Tides of War by Marcus Turner
The Jindabyne Secret by Jo Hart
River of Diamonds by S. M. Isaac
Salvaged by C.A. Clark
Emoto's Promise by Shel Calopa

RIVER OF DIAMONDS

S.M. ISAAC

DROWNED EARTH

First published by Deadset Press in 2020

www.aussiespeculativefiction.com

ISBN: 978-0-6484211-9-1

Cover design Copyright © Alanah Andrews

Edited by Alanah Andrews & Austin P. Sheehan

www.aussiespeculativefiction.com

DEDICATION

To my husband and my son,

With all the love in the world.

CHAPTER ONE: TEMPEST

A ladybird the size of a bottle cap tickled the fine hair on Rosa's arm, and her eyes flew open. She peered at the beetle and noted the mutated amphibious webbing along its tiny hind legs. They didn't need to spend time in water, so why were they growing unnecessary parts?

She watched the ladybird crawl across her hand. It was rarer to find normal bugs than mutants lately. Everyone said the world had changed since the waters had risen, they always said it with a sigh as if remembering better days. Rosa hadn't known any other world, but the changes happening in front of her, like the amphibious ladybirds, were unsettling.

"If you're going to ignore me, Rosella—"

Rosa jumped, suddenly noticing the man sitting beside her in the back seat of the car.

"—I'll get going. It's been what, eight months since I saw you last and you're still carelessly sleeping out here alone. Use that smart head of yours for something other than reading and tinkering with useless junk for once. Anyone could find you, and then . . ." Greg shook his head, but Rosa saw his hand twitch above the machete at his side.

She cast a wary eye over him while attempting to regain her composure. A giant hunting knife was fastened to Greg's left boot, but the straps over his shoulders where his shotgun usually hung were empty. His grey-streaked beard hadn't been trimmed for some time—he must have come straight to see her before his tyres had cooled from travel.

"Eight months and two days," she said, "and the same old argument as if you'd never left." She pretended to fiddle with the buttons on her shirt, checking the treasure in her pocket. Rosa had awaited Greg's return with both impatience and trepidation. She always missed him, but this time was different. This time, Rosa had found something that could change their lives, maybe even change the whole country, forever. But Greg came in here without even a hello or asking her about her progress on the project in the corner of her workshop, so her treasure would have to wait. "Where's your shotgun?" she asked. "You took it off to sneak in here, didn't you? You wanted to catch me unaware. Were you spoiling for a fight?"

"Do you ever listen to what I teach you?" asked Greg, sighing. "Not all mutant wildlife are as seemingly harmless as the ladybirds. The Wild Dogs aren't make-believe, either. They *decimate* settlements. What if I'm on the other side of the country when something happens? I'd come back to find you gone." He reached out and ran his gloved fingers through Rosa's hair.

She pulled her head away. "No-one comes in here," said Rosa. "But just in case, I always have my ratchet handy, so if I needed to I could conk someone on the head."

Greg caught her wrist, the ratchet hovering inches from his forehead. "You'd conk a gang member on the head, would you? Just like that? Wouldn't matter if he had a gun or was stronger than you?" His grip tightened.

She yanked her wrist but couldn't extricate it from Greg's strong grasp, so she leaned forward to get right in his face. "Your annual lessons won't keep me alive, Greg. It's me out here, just me. I can handle myself."

With a gentle twist, Greg disarmed her and

handed the tool back with a sad smile. "Are you sure, Birdie?"

Rosa thrust the ratchet into her belt and turned away from him.

"Righto," he said, "I get it. I'm not your bodyguard. If you're going to put yourself in such idiotic situations, then I'm done. I don't need another Joy."

Rosa shrank inwardly. She couldn't even think of asking Greg to help her now. His partner, Joy, had died out there.

"I don't have time for this," said Greg. He placed a small parcel wrapped in a clean red cloth on the seat between them. "Happy Christmas." He got out and made his way amongst the salvaged cars.

Curiosity piqued, Rosa unfolded the parcel, wrinkling her nose as the grease on her fingers rubbed off onto the clean wrapping. A grille emblem with six stars fell into her palm. It had been polished and mounted on a small metal cone. Her star. Rosa smiled. She had searched for a star emblem for years to top her Christmas tree of salvaged hood ornaments.

Rosa got out of the car and jogged after Greg. She caught him in a hug before he had time to strap his shotgun on. "I missed you."

Greg pulled her close. "I missed you too, Birdie."

She breathed in the leather and gun oil and

crushed oak scent that was Greg. This was her moment to tell him what she had found and ask him to come with her . . .

Aire's alarm bells sounded. Three times.

Rosa's heart raced as her head ran the kilometre from her workshop to the village. Alarms sounded only for a severe storm, and three bells meant a superstorm. Joe, the resident weather-reader, had never been wrong about an incoming tempest. She didn't know if they would make it in time, but they couldn't weather the storm in her workshop—too many loose objects could easily become deadly missiles.

"Let's go," she said, tearing out of Greg's embrace. "We need to get to the village. Now."

The wind whipped around them as they ran. Rosa tasted the storm on her tongue like warm, salted earth. During a storm was the only time she wished for her workshop to be closer to the village. She ran faster, listening for Greg's heavy footfalls to make sure he was keeping pace.

"I've always weathered storms in the ute," Greg yelled over the wind as they approached his canopied utility vehicle. "I'm staying here, not going to the top of a bloody tree."

Rosa swore. She turned around and grabbed his arm. "Not three-bells, Greg! You know the protocols, stop wasting time!"

Greg nodded reluctantly. He followed without further prompting when the storm clouds roiled, an ominous backdrop come to life, enveloping the forest like a fog.

They climbed the stairs to the suspended walkway that was the thoroughfare of Aire. The village had been a tourist attraction before the Rise, a treetop walk in a forest of myrtle beech, blackwood and the occasional mountain ash. Twelve tower rooms and myriad tree-houses accommodated the forty-odd residents. Rosa's father had founded the village in the crown of the forest on the premise that the waters would continue to rise, and one day, reach them.

As they sprinted towards the tower rooms, loose branches began to detach, threatening to trip them up or knock them over. They would be blown away before they reached the common room in the second tower. Rosa's room was just ahead of them. She swung the door open and threw herself inside, Greg barrelling in behind her. She secured the door and helped him fasten the window shutters.

"Is your room big enough?" puffed Greg. "I mean, will the tree bend more if there's two of us in here?"

"This is one of the sturdiest rooms we've got.

Lock your shotgun and knives in the wardrobe."

Greg removed his weapons as the roomed creaked and groaned, and Rosa secured the few loose objects in the room, including her Christmas tree. She lit the olive-oil lamp secured in a small metal cage bolted to the floor, casting the room in a warm glow. There was little to do during a storm, and pacing and fretting weren't high on her list, though they appeared to be on Greg's.

"Sit," she said. "You're not helping."

"How do you do this, Birdie?" he said, bracing himself against the wall. "The whole room's moving."

"They've been getting worse."

"Helpful," said Greg. "That's the most helpful thing you could have said to me right now. Cheers for that." He took off his shirt and rolled it into a ball, then looked around for somewhere to put it. The t-shirt underneath stuck to his chest.

Rosa sat on the bed and crossed her legs to stop from fidgeting. The storms were frightening and despite the lamp-light, they enveloped all the senses. This was the first time in a long while she had weathered one with company. "Here," she said, "come sit. Let's talk about something else."

She smoothed down the blanket, trying to filter the roar of the wind out of her agitated thoughts. No time like the present to ask for Greg's help, but doubts crowded her mind. Mentioning her plan's world-changing potential sounded juvenile, even if it was the truth. Greg was twice her age, and sometimes he acted like she was a child who had gotten into trouble when he was gone.

"If I wanted to go somewhere," she said carefully, "somewhere outside Aire, would you come with me?"

Greg raised an eyebrow at her. He sat on the edge of the bed, though he remained rigid. "You mean like a holiday, or you want to become a trader? Is that what the car's for?"

So he *had* looked in the corner of her workshop. "I'll ignore that you poked your nose under the tarp without asking," she said, and the corner of Greg's mouth quirked up. "No, I mean to look for something that might help lots of people."

Greg threw back his head and laughed. A normal laugh that showed he had temporarily forgotten about the storm. "You want to go treasure hunting? What have you been reading now? Most people are looking for exactly what you have here in Aire. You won't have far to go."

"A kind of treasure, I suppose," said Rosa, shifting closer to him and tucking loose strands of hair behind her ears. "If I get my hands on it, I'll be able to study it, to reverse engineer the tech and—"

"You're serious?" said Greg, his laughter replaced by the howling wind. "Exactly what sort of treasure?"

Rosa stared at Greg for long seconds. "Water. Reverse osmosis filters."

Her eyes never left Greg's. She fancied she could feel his heart beating, though it was just hers beating hard enough for the both of them.

"I've heard about the communities out there," she continued, buoyed by his lack of immediate rejection. "I know how much they need fresh water. I've found a way to help them."

Greg rubbed his eyebrow. "You have nothing packed in your car to deal with that, and not enough provisions besides, unless these filters are within the forest boundaries."

Rosa grunted, but then nodded grudgingly. "Noted. What do you say?"

Greg clapped his hands together. "Right, if you want me to go with you, you'll do it my way. Ask Frannie's permission, stock up properly and show me that darn map you've been trying to hide."

Rosa's mouth fell open. Frustration, affront, a bit of awe flashed into her head, but she landed on anger. "You know Ma Frannie will never give me permission to go."

"That settles it, then. We're not going."

Rosa narrowed her eyes. "You think you can control everything, don't you?"

"And you don't?"

Rosa glared at him.

"Look, I am the authority out there," he said, with no hint of a boast. "It would be wise to take my advice."

Rosa's minimal furniture shuddered against the walls despite being strapped down. The tang of seawater and a mouldy, earthy smell blew in, overwhelming the normal crisp forest scent.

"I know what you're doing," said Greg, raising his voice over the wind, "and I should be comforting you."

Greg's change of mood caught Rosa off-guard. "Why?" she asked. "Because I'm a woman who becomes hysterical in storms?" She flung her head back dramatically. "Oh, save me from the lightning and thunder!"

Greg smiled, then laughed. Rosa joined in.

"No," he said, "because I'm older and I protect people. It's what I do." His smile fell. Rosa saw the anguish in his eyes.

She squeezed Greg's thigh, then pulled him up

the bed until their backs rested against the wall. She lay her head on his chest and closed her eyes when he put an arm around her. The gale roared around them, and the little room shook and moved and groaned.

Greg's head slid onto hers, but sleep was a long time coming for Rosa. And it had nothing to do with the storm.

CHAPTER TWO: AIRE

Rosa woke to an empty room. "Greg?"

It was eerily silent. She opened the shuttered windows to thick morning fog. The storm had abated.

Her stomach knotted as she remembered last night's conversation with Greg. No-one likes holes being poked in their plans, even if the holes were there from the beginning. In her sleepless hours resting against Greg's shoulder, breathing in his scent mingled with the storm's sharpness, Rosa had made her decision. She would leave to find her treasure. Today.

She rested her hand on the map in the pocket next to her heart. It belonged there, a symbol of hope for her—and everyone else's—future.

"Rosa, you good?" Joe stuck his head into the room. He nodded when he saw Rosa, but not in greeting. She knew he was ticking off the list of residents and rooms in his head. "You're the last. All is well." He left before she could ask where Greg was.

Greg wasn't a citizen of Aire but had been invited years ago by one of the village's original salvaging team. As a trader, he was a necessary part of making sure that the citizens of Aire were thriving, and not just surviving. The village produced what it could, salvaged for necessities it couldn't grow, and traded for extra supplies.

Rosa picked her way along the walkways strewn with broken branches and debris. All the structures looked intact, if windblown. It had been a dry storm despite the smell of seawater. They had been lucky.

Greg wasn't in the common room. He was probably sitting somewhere waiting for her to find him, so Rosa dawdled while making her tea. She plucked mint leaves from the hydroponic garden, one of many circling the tower rooms and supplying Aire with an abundance of fresh food. Mint and eucalyptus tea—her favourite.

She found Greg sitting with his feet hanging over the side of a bridge. He never worried about being twenty-five metres off the ground—as long as the wind wasn't blowing. His hands were curled around a mug, and his face was at peace. He looked years younger. She stifled her relieved smile in case he was looking and sat next to him, settling her shoulder against his.

The mist hung thick and damp, but refreshingly so after the humid night spent enclosed. Apart from Greg, and the rope in front of her, all was cloud.

"It's peaceful after a storm," said Rosa.

Greg sipped from his mug and a sharp scent shot up Rosa's nose. She grunted disgustedly. "You should try tea sometime."

He grinned. "After that gale, I needed something stiff, but seeing as this is my second . . . Okay, let's swap. But you're not allowed to chuck it over the side or else I'll send you over after it."

They swapped drinks. Rosa took a tentative sip and scrunched her nose. "Just drink from the petrol tank why don't you?"

Greg chuckled. "It's not scotch, but it burns the right way."

"Where did you have scotch?"

"There's a little place up nor-east that has some special stuff. Called The Well."

"The Well? Okay, your turn."

Greg made a big act of wafting the steam towards him before taking a delicate sip. "It tastes like tree."

Rosa snorted over her mug and immediately regretted it when her eyes started to water. "I hope the workshop's okay. I'll check once the fog's lifted." She hoped her project car was still intact. "How long are you staying?"

Greg's pause was so small, Rosa thought she had imagined it. "I was thinking until the New Year."

Rosa's ears perked. Staying for that long was pretty much settling down for the mercenary. She pushed the thought away. It wouldn't matter, because she was leaving.

"It's been a long time since I've had a break," he continued, "and Frannie offered me a room since she was thrilled with the eggs and oranges I brought her. Sorry about the brake fluid, though. I would have brought some if I'd known Mack hadn't come past. He was due a couple of months ago—you haven't seen him at all?"

Rosa frowned. "I've got enough brake fluid to tide me over, but no, we haven't." Mack was the only other trader apart from Greg who knew the location of Aire. Greg's referral had gotten him in, but he was restricted to certain sections of the village—Mack had never even glimpsed their water tanks.

Greg shifted, but said nothing, staring into the fog.

Rosa fought with her own thoughts. How could her mother, the matriarch of the village, remain so secretive? Aire had water. Aire was self-sufficient. Aire could give aid but chose not to.

Was she making the right decision in leaving? Despite being acutely aware of the different set of rules out there, Rosa still hated the lies they lived. She would never betray Aire, but every day she stayed, her honesty and integrity wisped away. It mattered that Aire was flourishing when there was an entire world out there struggling to survive.

The map in her pocket would solve so much. Clean water—for everyone. A prototype to model future endeavours on. Perhaps even a new settlement—her own settlement that would be open to anyone who needed help.

She was definitely making the right decision.

"It is a blessing to be off the radar," said Greg carefully. "You wouldn't want what's out there to come in here."

They sipped as they sat amongst the clouds.

"I could get used to this, Birdie."

***

Rosa attached the safety line to the walkway's steel railing and hopped over the side.

After a storm, Rosa was responsible for checking the main water tanks concealed within each tower, a job that forced her thoughts to her father each time. He had always attended to the duties at hand before anything else, and she had always admired his dedication. She would see to her duties before leaving Aire.

Rosa's father had set up the units with filtration systems the year before he died. Rosa had been with him every step of the way, and she knew them inside and out, as he had intended. While he fitted each one, he had shared his dreams with her. "One day," he said, "we'll find some reverse osmosis filters, and we'll build a plant together. We'll reverse engineer the tech, and then we'll be able to open the doors to Aire."

Rosa had replied, "And then the world."

Rosa's mind wandered to her map. One day . . .

"Storms are messy," said Frannie from the walkway above. "Mister Valley, you're a sweetie for offering to help. You make an old woman happy."

"It's the least I can do," said Greg. Rosa imagined his big grin at the compliment.

She sighed. Of course, it's the last two people she wanted to see. She considered waiting until they left, but when her mother got chatty, seasons could pass. Then she heard her name.

"Rosa's planning something foolhardy," said Greg. "She's stocked that car of hers and is going out to find a desalination plant. She wants the filters—"

"Those filters," Frannie made a rude sound, "still haunting me. She's her father's daughter."

"Let her go, Frannie. She'll likely leave when I'm not around, otherwise."

"It's a fool's errand, but harm can come to her, regardless. I know you'll do everything you can, but I can't give my permission knowing she'll get hurt—I would never forgive myself."

Greg grunted. "You've put me in a hard place, then."

"Your ute," Frannie continued as if they hadn't just discussed Rosa, "is in pieces all over. I'm sorry. At least you'll get to stay for our Christmas Eve feast this year—it's the only time we go all out, and I'm cooking. Morning honey," she said, as Rosa climbed over the railing. At least Greg had the grace to blush. "I wish you would have taken to cooking, though too many cooks spoil the dish, as they say. Your father would be proud of you though, and I wouldn't have it any other way."

Rosa smiled, but it was brittle. She ran her finger over the workshop key in her pocket. She wanted to check the water tanks, pack her car and leave.

"You do this on your own?" Greg asked, eyeing her safety wire.

"Sometimes," said Rosa. "How did you think I checked the tanks?"

"You're stupid. And Frannie," he said, turning to her mother, "you should know better."

"Don't you go changing anything!" said Rosa, brandishing the hook from her line at him. "It's fine the way it is."

"He's just concerned for you, honey," said Frannie. "Why don't you let him join you if it makes him feel better?" She waved them away. "Nothing's more important to our way of life than water," she said, "except for making me some grandkids, so take your time. Especially after a storm when we've been reminded what we could lose."

"Ma, no!" said Rosa, blushing.

"Greg's a fine choice," continued Frannie, "it's about time you stopped mooning over him and took some action."

Greg chuckled heartily, following Rosa as she stalked away. Frannie hadn't made life easy for her being the only unattached woman. She continually foisted Clive into her path, thinking that as the next most mechanically minded person in the village, Rosa would be attracted to him. Clive was a hoot to be around, but Rosa didn't appreciate Frannie's interference, or that she seemed to be placing the entire future of Aire's population on her only daughter.

At the next tower room, Rosa attached the safety

line and hopped over the side as usual. She may have hopped more exuberantly for shock value, but she was used to the routine.

The look Greg gave her when she climbed back onto the walkway turned her smile into a cringe.

She finished her rounds quickly and made her way amongst the ferns and moss-covered tree trunks to her shed. What if the storm had damaged her car? The thought hounded her. She walked right past Greg's ute and had to double back when Greg stopped to look it over. It wasn't as damaged as Frannie had made out, but it was battered beyond easy repair.

"I could fix it—"

"Something will turn up," said Greg, cutting her off. A frown creased his face as he took in the destruction, but he didn't linger.

Rosa slid open the shed door and exhaled the breath she didn't realise she'd been holding. A large piece of siding had pulled loose and tree branches, leaves, and clods of dirt covered the floor. It looked like half the forest had blown in.

"Oh no . . ." She tore off the tarp that had tangled around her project car's side mirror. Greg made a pile with the larger debris while she methodically checked her car for damage.

Clive, the head salvager at Aire, had brought back

the Impreza WRX from one of his expeditions for her to restore—though it had been missing her coveted star emblems. He had fluked finding the beaut, and an entire boot-load of spare parts, in a garage three years ago on an inland salvage job. Someone had taken great pains to get it ready for rallying—she had found a competition rules booklet in the glove-box—so it had a roll-cage, powertrain and suspension mods, and a safety fuel cell. It had only needed the regular fuel burn-off to get the nasties out from sitting around so long, and a flush of some fluids, and it was as good as ever.

"Well, don't leave me in suspense," said Greg after a few minutes.

Rosa rested her forehead on the C-pillar and closed her eyes for a moment. Then she turned around and smiled. "She's going to be fine—a couple of dings, but otherwise, fine."

Branches crunched outside, announcing Clive's ute. There was a dull thump as he ran into the wall at slow speed.

"Sorry, Rosa, told you it was the brakes," said Clive through his window, a big grin twitching his ginger-flecked beard. "Merc." He nodded at Greg.

They pushed the ute inside the workshop. Rosa had forgotten Clive had asked her to take a look at it.

"I'll leave you to it, love," said Clive. "I've got to

rustle up the others to help with clean up before we head out tomorrow. Could be gone close to a month. Anything you need this time around?"

"Sure is," said Rosa, taking the keys from him and smiling her most endearing smile. "I need to come with you to make sure you get the right parts." It was their usual routine, Rosa insisting she needed to come salvaging, and Clive saying it was too dangerous.

Clive's grin returned. "Soon, love. Your Ma would have my hide. It isn't a place out there for, well, anyone really." He nodded towards Greg. "The Merc will corroborate. The Wild Dogs have been about. I even saw one of the snarling dogs painted on a settlement after they'd been through. On what was left, at any rate."

Clive shook his head. "It's all right, the Wardens are out there, too. Wouldn't mind a bunch of mysterious do-gooders helping out. Someone's got to clean up the mess out there when there's no gov to do it."

Rosa snorted. "Don't tell me you believe they're protectors?"

"I've seen plenty of people swear by the Wardens, love. They bring closure, a sense of security in their own right. Even if I don't know the half of what they do, I stand by something that does some good."

"They aren't the saviours of the wasteland," she said, slamming her palms onto Clive's bonnet. "They're vile, their hands are just as bloody as the Dogs'. Chaining someone in a container in the middle of the desert is a death sentence. What right do the Wardens have to judge?"

Greg stepped forward and gently touched the back of Rosa's hand. "Hating something you don't understand is how villains are made, Rosa. Would you let all the criminals walk free? They have up to a week to repent or make peace with their crimes—more than most of them deserve. These aren't just petty thieves, these are people who have slaughtered entire families—or worse. The Wardens aren't just anyone either, you know. They're—"

"They're just human, like us," said Rosa. "They're not all-knowing."

"I suppose you're right in that," said Greg quietly.

Rosa turned on her heel and set about working on Clive's ute. Greg continued to clear out the storm debris.

"I'll be back soon," called Clive on his way out the door.

The pair worked in peace until Greg appeared beside Rosa as she was bleeding the brakes. "Why do you want to leave the village so much, Rosa? Aire's the nicest darned place on Earth. What more do you want?"

"Sure it's nice." Rosa pumped the brake pedal. It

was still far too spongy. "I like having my own space, the resources to tinker with things. I know my abilities aren't particularly useful to the village—apart from knowing about the tanks—and I do try to help out, but I hear whispers about why I can't fix a door or a broken bridge. Everyone expects me . . . they expect me to be my father. How can I live up to that? Da gave his life to Aire. He pitched in everywhere."

Greg sighed, leaning against the car. "Not disputing it, Birdie, but that doesn't mean your skills aren't valued in Aire."

Rosa snorted and flicked a rag at Greg's hip so he would get off the car. Everyone in their community performed a specific role but, out of necessity, they helped with other tasks. However, it seemed no-one was as inept at anything quite like Rosa was at carpentry.

"Is that why you want to leave?" asked Greg, leaning down and rubbing a bit of grease off Rosa's forehead with his sleeve. "You shouldn't care that much about what people think of you. I have strong suspicions you would be missed."

"Their suspicions are suffocating!" Rosa threw the rag on the ground. "They don't help anyone outside of their perfect village. There's so much going on out there, so many people needing help. How can they not do anything?"

"Anyone out there would take advantage of Aire," said Greg. "Your people are protecting their own. It's what people have done throughout the history of the world."

"What about heroes? There's got to be heroes out there. I want to change the world, Greg, not hide away."

"The heroes are all dead, Rosa."

Rosa pumped the brake pedal harder than she needed to. The tension was back, so at least she didn't put the pedal, and her foot, through the floor.

"All good, Rosa?" called Clive.

"Thought you said no-one ever comes in here?" said Greg, looking towards the door, "But Clive seems to feel at home."

Rosa hopped out to meet Clive, leaving Greg standing there. Her legs were all wobbly.

"You're back quickly," said Rosa.

"I don't muck around," he said. "Ma Frannie's already got the clean-up in full swing, and the salvage crew are on stand-by. Just need the wheels." He glanced at the ute. "Unless you need more time?"

Rosa threw him the keys. "Brakes are good to go."

"You sure are handy with the tools," said Clive, grinning. "No more crashing for me." He glanced at

Greg. "Merc, have a word?"

Greg eyed Rosa before stepping outside. She waited a moment and then tiptoed over to the door and listened in.

"We ain't expecting no trouble, Merc," said Clive. "Place doesn't need you."

"Might be a time soon I'll be here more than you are," said Greg. "Something you'll have to get used to."

"I gave her that there car in the corner," said Clive, more quietly. "What do you give her? A heart attack every time you show up alive?"

"I'm not having this out with you here," said Greg.

Rosa heard enough. She stalked over to her project car. The little she needed to take was already stowed in the car's boot, including some well-chosen spare parts. She spent most of her time in the workshop, so no-one had questioned when she took food, clothes, water, and a few extra jerry cans of fuel.

There were only the most important items left to pack. Her tools. She picked up a satchel and set about packing her favourite tools into it, those most useful all-round. It was difficult to condense them in such a way, and the reality of what she was doing sunk in. She was nervous, but finally acting out her plans was exhilarating.

Rosa looked over her workshop one last time, her

eyes lingering on her father's mechanical manuals. They were too cumbersome to take, though they were the hardest to leave. If she came back for anything, it would be those.

Rosa opened the door to her project car and whispered goodbye to her workshop.

"You leaving without me?"

"Greg!" Rosa hit her head on the door frame as she jumped and whirled around in fright.

Greg leaned against her car. "I noticed you took the star."

Her heart hammered in her chest as she looked at the workshop door. Clive was gone and so was his ute. She had been so absorbed by her packing that she didn't hear him leave.

"Are you going to turn me in?" she demanded. "That's it, isn't it? You want to make sure I'm bound and gagged and stuck in this place forever." She mentally calculated her chances of leaving if Greg didn't want her to. She wouldn't even be able to get the key in the ignition.

"Are you done?" He looked thoughtful but grim. "I could destroy the map right now, could stop you if I wanted to. You have endless room in your brain for all this technical stuff, and—for some reason—ladybirds, but sometimes you lack a shred of sense. What do you want, Rosa?"

Rosa lifted her chin. "I found a map to a desalination plant in an old Melways," she said. "I want to follow it, and I want you to come with me."

Greg raised an eyebrow. "And how's a desal plant meant to help the world?"

"Maybe not the world to start with, but—" Rosa noticed that Greg had his full arsenal on him today. Even his pack. His traders pack. "Where are *you* going?"

"As much as I would love for you to stay here where it's safe," he said, "and believe me I considered keeping you here—"

Rosa's smile could have set a dormant fruit tree to blossom. "You're coming with me."

"Now, don't you get all happy," said Greg. "You'll have to show me the map, tell me your plans, and when they're chock-a-block with flaws, you'll take my advice. Your first mistake was even considering going alone—that's the number one rule out there and you know it, don't go anywhere alone."

"What about focusing on the good it will do if the plan works?"

Greg shook his head. "That's not how you survive, Birdie, and you need to survive to get there first."

Rosa took Greg's pack from him and stowed it behind the front seat. "I made the same mods Clive requests for his ute to prepare for whatever's out there," she said, unable to hide her enthusiasm. "I lifted the suspension, swapped the under-tray for a steel protection plate, and I installed a compressed air system as . . . Hold on," she said, looking into the boot. "You've been in my car." It was full of extra bags, and everything was tied down symmetrically with occy straps.

"Provisioning is taken care of," said Greg. "Let's see the map."

Rosa placed a hand protectively on her pocket. "Can I just tell you it's along the coast and navigate for you?"

"What do you think I'm going to do, Birdie, tear it to pieces?"

Rosa closed the boot, nearly catching Greg's fingers.

"Hey," said Greg, "come on now. If it's along the coast, the map's from before the Rise. The desal plant will be underwater. Besides, there's good reason to stay away from the coast. Have I told you the time I saw—"

"The octopus, yes," said Rosa. "It was as big as a cow and you hit it with your ute and the ink went everywhere, ruined half your stock. You've told me several times."

"And when we got out to check on it, we had to fight the thing that had gone berserk, and we weren't even close to the coast. There are all sorts of nasties near the edge, human and not. It's too unpredictable. What will you do if we find a Super Octopus, Rosa?"

"That's why you're part of my plan. You have first-hand experience with vicious cephalopods."

"I suppose those were in your encyclopaedia too? I mean it. What's your plan? You'll need diving gear, and what on earth are you going to use to remove the filters?"

Rosa put a foot in the driver's door and looked over the roof at Greg. "Get in."

"You're yanking my chain, right?" said Greg, staring as if she had asked him to get into a miniature toy instead of her car. "It's red."

"I'm sorry it didn't come in another colour at the dealership . . . Hey, what are you doing? Don't you dare!"

Greg was shaking two cans of automotive paint. "It's too nice, Birdie, we'll be a beacon to everything and everyone who sees us. I thought you were going to fix it up before we left. We need to ugly it up, camouflage it."

Greg started spraying the paint over the roof— he'd grabbed brown and navy blue—without a care for sealing the windows or keeping the colours separate.

With a strangled cry, Rosa grabbed a handful of rags and rubbed at the roof. She shoved some more rags at Greg with one hand while trying to poke the rest in the window crack to save the glass of her beautiful car. "You,

you . . . mongrel chicken!" She threw the rags on the floor and hit him on the shoulder. Then she pummelled him some more.

"Mongrel chicken?" Greg laughed. "Out of all the insults you could have used." He sighed. "You really aren't ready to go out there." He held out a can. "Here, help me camo this."

Rosa, sullen, helped Greg vandalise her car. It was a rough job, but no red was left when they finished.

"Ready?" said Rosa.

A long, wailing siren sounded. It could only be Aire's alarm, but it wasn't one she had ever heard before.

Greg took out his shotgun and seemed to change into the Otway panther of legend, crouching low and moving swiftly, silently, and deadly. "And here I was hoping to have one last cup of tea."

CHAPTER THREE: THE OUTBACK

Rosa picked up a hefty spanner and peeked around the door. She couldn't see Greg—or any sign of a storm. The sky was clear apart from a few innocuous clouds and barely a breeze to move her long hair. She walked around the side of the shed.

The smell of smoke accosted her. Plumes rose high above the treetops over the village. One side of her shed faced a partial clearing, so the road was visible for almost five hundred metres amongst the dotted trees from where she stood, though her shed was hidden to anyone driving past. At the edge of the clearing were two unfamiliar white utes with something black scrawled across their bonnets. She ran towards them, spurred by shock.

A figure darted out at her, but she didn't have enough time to cry out as she was scooped up and flung into a hollow. Rosa crashed down onto whoever held her, and the wind was knocked out of her. She tried to roll off, but the arms pinned hers tightly. She still didn't have enough breath to scream.

"Rosa, it's me," said Greg from beneath her. He said it over and over until she stopped struggling and finally understood the words.

She rolled off and turned to face him.

"You need to go," he said before she could gather words. "Start the car and drive out of here. I'll find you after I make sure everything's okay."

Rosa gripped her spanner, the adrenalin still coursing through her, confusing her thoughts. "What's happening? I can't just leave now—"

"You can't help here. In fact, if they see you, it'll make things worse. Trust me on this. You wanted to go, go. I promise I will do everything I can. I'll find you before you reach the edge of the forest. Now, go. Run."

Rosa made to follow him but he turned and loomed over her. His voice was almost a growl, "You will make things worse. It's the Wild Dogs, they take women like you. Go to the car and drive. I *will* find you."

Rosa started towards her car reluctantly, then bolted when the siren stopped. For some reason, it was worse without it wailing.

This wasn't how she planned on leaving Aire.

She drove along the narrow track, thick undergrowth brushing her car. The canopy filtered out most of the sunlight, so everything was damp and vibrant. Evidence of the recent storm was everywhere. Split trunks, splintered branches, whole trees ripped out by their roots.

It was slow going. In order to protect Aire, the villagers planted misleading trails, debris, even transplanted noxious shrubs to confuse and deter people who ventured into the forest. Rosa knew to follow the main trail and persist in moving, and then replacing, the fallen trees in her path. She left any storm damage to the side. At the third such stop, the tracks and battered shrubs caused by the Dogs' utes on their way in became obvious. They hadn't bothered with the trees, nor had the false trails tricked them. A troubling thought.

A wallaby moved in the bushes, craning its head to look at her. Out of habit, she studied it. She found what she hadn't known she was looking for—webbed claws. Another superfluous mutation. She moved another branch of storm-felled debris out of her path, worried she would tire before she reached the edge of the forest. She considered following the Dogs' trail out, but Clive and his crew would already have a hard time fixing it. Besides, what if there were more of them?

Footfalls approached, and she grasped the branch as a weapon, determined to protect herself. Her arms trembled.

Greg charged into view. His clothes were roughed and dirty, and his face and knuckles bloody.

"All the villagers are alive," said Greg without preamble. Rosa nodded gratefully. "They damaged the first two tower rooms and some outlying tree-houses—including yours. I'm sorry. They didn't get any further in before they were stopped. Luckily there weren't many of them—I don't think they actually expected to find anything, though how they knew to get as far as they did . . ." Greg shook his head, his features becoming dark.

Rosa finally found her voice. "Do you think it was Mack?" She didn't want to believe it of the trader, but what other explanation was there? She hesitated. "Will more come?"

Greg's mouth set into a grim line. He didn't say anything, but he didn't have to. There was no way to be sure about either possibility.

They drove, moving debris as needed until they came to the forest limits. The trees concealing the entrance had been flung aside, baring the forest to the world. Rosa brought the car to an idle, helping Greg cover the entrance. Then she gazed out at the barren landscape. She was about to cross into unfamiliar territory. Her point of no return. She would have savoured the moment if not for the worry in the pit of her stomach.

"What did you tell them about me?" she asked.

"That you were okay," said Greg. "That we were leaving to do something important, but that I'd be with you. Clive didn't much like the second part."

The storm had hit the fields hard, too. Water pooled and drowned the meagre plant life—bracken bushes and the skeletal remains of trees. Rosa's stomach churned. She felt Greg's hand on her arm and realised she must have made some noise or movement that indicated her discomfit.

"I'm not turning back," she said, to herself or Greg, she wasn't sure.

"Pull over," said Greg.

"I just said—"

"We're not turning back, yes, but you're about to drive into a bog, so pull over. I should drive from here. I know the roads, and the marshland is hard to navigate if you haven't done it before. It would be far too easy to get stuck."

Greg rubbed his face and knuckles with a wet cloth before taking over. The areas of marsh were murky and blended so well with the ochre-coloured dirt Rosa would have driven straight into them, though Greg avoided them deftly.

"So, tell me about the air compressor you added to the car," said Greg, his voice unusually chipper.

"Thank you, but you don't need to pretend to be interested."

"That's what people do, Birdie, they ask questions, show interest, when they know the other person cares about something."

Rosa would have loved to tell Greg in exciting detail the story of each part she had fitted to the car, but she settled for what he asked for. "Okay," she said. "I was trying to piece together an alternative fuel system for when the fuel runs out—for when all the fuel in the country runs out, I mean. I've added a small compressed air motor as a backup, but that meant I also needed a small on-board generator and a tank of compressed air, as well as an air compressor to fill it with. The project spiralled, but in the end, it's only a backup to the fuel because if we actually need to use it, the top speed isn't much more than a bicycle."

"But you got it working," said Greg. "You're a darned good mechanic, Birdie."

Rosa smiled, her heart lighter. Clouds of insects buzzed over the marshes, and her smile faltered. The plants were squat and bristled, or had tendrils snaking along to choke other plants. One of the trees moved and Rosa almost jumped out of her seat. It was a monitor lizard clawing the side of a white stump. The size of the monitor was incredible. Was it growing the same webbing as the ladybirds or the wallabies? She wasn't game enough to check.

"We're well out of Aire now," said Greg, "you've had your little taste of freedom. It's time to tell me your plan."

Rosa nodded. "I intend to salvage the reverse osmosis filters from the desal plant and rig them up somewhere to create a new system. Should be like changing a wheel."

Greg whistled. "Firstly, never mention the plant in front of anyone but me. Desal plants are considered gov territory. Secondly, you've never seen reverse osmosis filters before. Do you even know what else you'll need? I know you're a brilliant mechanic and you know a bit about the water tanks, but you're not exactly a water treatment technician. It seems a bit beyond reach."

"The map showed an old industrial area near the plant. We could take the filters anywhere, but I figured we'd have more luck with a factory. I'm sure there'll be components we need. I'm good at figuring things out. It may take some trial and error, but with the filters, I know I can do it."

"Rosa," said Greg, choosing his words carefully, "you'll need to fabricate the system, and not to bring up a sore subject, but that sort of thing has never been your strong point. Let's say you do manage it, then what'll we do? Create a settlement around the new plant and live happily ever after? This experiment could take years—decades."

"We're already well on our way, now." She shrugged.

"You're kidding me?" said Greg. "That's the whole plan? What if there's nothing to find, Rosella? We'll be stuck in the back of beyond!" He slapped the wheel. "Sometimes I don't know how to take you. Are you a cheeky little pup that needs to be swatted, or are you a brilliant tactician planning each move? Before we left, I'd already decided to see this through with you, so you can quit being sneaky with me from now on. As for me, I'm done being the patient mentor. You've been warned."

They left the marshland behind and suddenly the earth was dry and cracked, the car bumping over the ground instead of sinking. The vegetation remained offensive, though now it looked sickly, too. Brown spots, powdery growths, cracks. Was it a reaction to the extreme weather? She hoped it wasn't anything more sinister—something akin to the creepy superfluous mutations on the animals. It was common knowledge the coastal waters were toxic to some degree—perhaps it was slowly being brought inland?

"It's like this everywhere," said Greg. "One minute you're in water, the next, a desert. It takes some getting used to. I grew up around here before the Rise."

Rosa's attention perked. Greg rarely spoke of his childhood.

"This was all farmland," he said. "Green fields filled with sheep, or yellow canola looking like the sun fallen to earth but smelling sweet and, to be honest, a bit rotten. There were hills and eucalyptus trees, farmhouses, tracks to muck around on in your paddock bombs."

"Paddock bombs?"

"Old cars, nasty condition, not good for anything but driving around until they die."

"Sounds like my kind of fun."

Rosa tried to imagine Greg's fields, yellow and green and soft, overlaying the pictures in her mind's eye to what was in front of her. The hills rolled out in dirty orange waves, with spiky grass amongst the ruts. If she squinted, the land smoothed, but it was the best she could do. The paddock bombs she could imagine better—they would have fun with them even in the current conditions, and she itched to take over driving to do a couple of doughnuts and gun it out over the hills.

A shape popped up on the horizon and Rosa squinted, trying to work out what it was. As they drew closer, she made out a blue shipping container with old canvas stretched across the top and over the front like a veranda. Was this one of the Wardens' containers?

She turned to Greg in a fluster. "What if there's someone inside?" she asked. "Can we free them? Is it true the Wardens leave the key to the shackles just out of reach? Would the Wardens track us down and shackle us in there if we *did* set them free?" Rosa was breathless when she finished.

"Calm down, Birdie," said Greg. "Of course someone's in there." He ignored the look of outrage on Rosa's face. "A vendor from the town not far beyond those hills. They take it in turns to sell their wares out here where the caravans drive past."

He slowed as they approached the container. A solitary man sat inside, brushing flies away from his face.

Greg leaned across Rosa and shouted out the window, "The sun sets on a quiet day that needs nothing more than news of what lies ahead."

The man brushed the flies away again in a useless effort and replied, "Nothing needed this quiet day. Only a Warden, but no Dogs have passed this way, and bare were his hands with nothing to say." He nodded and Greg returned the gesture before driving on.

Rosa turned to Greg with her eyebrows raised and the start of a grin on her face. "It's like something out of a story. What does it mean? Why do you—"

"Imagine sitting in a box all day with nothing to do. Be a bit like driving all day, every day. You'd start playing games in your head. Counting games, word games. The vendors started passing on their rhymes and codes to those relieving them. Now it's the way things are done. Those that frequently pass the box vendors play along. It's the only way to get info."

"Isn't he scared of the Dogs?" she asked.

"There's an unspoken rule that no-one harms the box vendors. They might supply you with the very thing you need to survive, even if it's just the news of what's ahead. At any rate, harming one would call down the wrath of the Wardens, and everyone wants to avoid that."

Rosa's mouth tightened.

A cloud of dust moved towards them and Greg pulled into a sparse copse of trees. He let the car idle as he inspected the approaching truck.

"Headlights work, yes?" he asked Rosa.

She gave him a thumbs-up, and Greg flicked the lights on and off in a sequence. The truck returned a three-one-one. Greg remained at ease so Rosa eyed the truck curiously as it pulled up next to their window. The driver, his long hair tied back into a braid, was not much older than Rosa.

"Will," said Greg, "good to see you, mate."

"Valley," said Will with a nod, "likewise. Scorcher out here today. Nothing happening in the Marsh, I take it?"

"Bang on. How about your way?"

Rosa opened her mouth to say something, but Greg squeezed her thigh to forestall her.

"Nothing to sook about, just the regular slog. Best keep on, night's coming."

"Hooroo," said Greg and drove off with a wave.

Behind them, Will pulled up to speak to the man in the container.

"That was an incredibly polite conversation," said Rosa sharply, pushing Greg's hand off her leg.

"I haven't forgotten about what happened," said Greg, "but we don't want to draw attention to Aire's part of the world. Always keep that in mind."

"How does anyone survive out here?" she asked. "Who do you trade with?"

"There are quite a few self-sufficient settlements," said Greg, "though none like yours. There are elitist settlements you couldn't get into if you had barrels of water strapped to your body. Then there's those so heavily coveted they change hands often and violently—tricky to anticipate a welcome in those. The best are those that require specific supplies and have their own produce or wares to trade. They do exist. Then there's those in the gov-state that were supplied water when they tried to ration it years ago. I wouldn't touch anything government, best to stay far away from that—it always comes with a cost. Trade is the best way. The black market stigma has faded. Anything non-gov is branded such, but there's barely a government anymore to—I digress. Aire's the best I've seen."

Rosa rolled her eyes, though Greg didn't see. What secrets were other settlements hiding? The settlement she was going to create would trade with everyone and wouldn't hide anything. It would be a deadset paradise.

"This is as far as I go without seeing the map," said Greg, looking for somewhere to stop. "I've humoured you and your secretive navigating long enough. I was hoping you would have offered the map to me because you trusted me, but now, you'll show it to me." His voice conveyed that he would see the map even if he had to pry it out of her hands.

"Can we keep going a little longer?" asked Rosa. "Zigzagging along these rough roads is taking longer than

I thought. I promise I'll show you the map in the morning."

"Didn't you make this thing outback tough? We're not keeping going, Birdie. There's a rest stop ahead. I don't like to get too close, but other traders will stop here too if they're close. If we used the headlights, every being out there, mutated or not, human or not, would come straight to us."

The clouds rolled in, bringing dusk early. Greg pulled into a ditch beside the road.

"Why are you afraid of showing me the map?" he asked.

Rosa looked at Greg's hands. An almighty bruise had formed on the knuckles on his right hand. "Because I'm sure there'll be another problem to add to the insurmountable list. There always is. I'll show you in the morning. I will."

Greg sighed, long and laboured. "I'll watch when it's dark," he said. "You can watch while it's still light, okay?"

"Sure," said Rosa, but when Greg opened the door, she caught his wrist. "Aren't you staying in the car?"

"Would you like to hold my hand in the bushes?" Rosa blushed and let go.

When he returned, she stepped away to take her

turn. She flipped him a rude gesture when he yelled after her, "Are you sure you don't want me to hold your hand?"

On her way back, she attached a small solar panel trickle charger to the battery to catch the last light. The battery, as it was for every car, was the biggest problem. Sitting so long unused made them worthless—it was one in a thousand that wouldn't have died after thirty years idle. Over the years, they had salvaged several battery reconditioning chargers that were able to carry out the reconditioning process on old batteries. With meticulous cycles of charging, they were able to keep a good store of batteries—albeit never at their best again.

They ate a dinner of cured kangaroo meat, root vegetables and dried fruit. Rosa reclined her seat. A breeze tickled her arm, and she looked around to see Greg's door ajar.

"Crack the window a little if you want fresh air," said Rosa.

"I prefer the door open," said Greg, adjusting his seat into a straight-backed position. "It's a warm night and it'll get humid in here without a breeze. Also, tin can closed up and all that. If someone sneaks up on us, I want to be able to move."

Rosa translated that as he would not sleep at all. She flicked out the interior light globe so it wouldn't place load on the battery.

Greg adjusted his knives and placed his shotgun on the dash within easy reach. "Sleep now, Birdie. I'm right here."

For the first time in her life, she was out in the world. For the first time in her life, she was following her heart. Possibilities ran through her mind. She reached over to rest her fingers lightly on Greg's arm. She drifted to sleep, content.

CHAPTER FOUR: DIAMONDS

A faint crying woke Rosa. Her skin prickled at the unexpected sound, and she looked through the fog of sleep for trouble. It was morning. Her sleep had been fitful without the rustle of leaves and the comforting sway she was accustomed to. Even the wind whistled differently on the ground than in the trees.

She leaned over, her cheek peeling off the headrest, seat creaking, and checked on Greg, who to her surprise, was asleep. She bounced on her seat, but he didn't flinch. She felt vaguely guilty for not allowing him the rest he'd planned on at Aire. She decided to let him sleep, take a quick peek and come back and get him if need be.

Rosa slipped out of the car and rested the door closed. All was still in the early light. She crouched and kept low in the ditch beside the road. The crying sounded close. She waited for several minutes before she mustered the courage to stand up and look across the road. She saw the old rest stop, tables and benches broken long ago. The billboard's faded advertisement told her to fly Qantas. Did planes still fly to Australia, somewhere far away from all the devastation?

Another cry came. A pile of rags next to a splintered bench moved. Was it a child? Rosa jogged across the road, startled into action. Who would abandon a child out here? As she neared, she realised the bundle was too big to be a child. She lay a hand on it even though it was caked with dried mud. "Are you okay?"

The bundle rolled over, whimpering. It was a man covered in grime.

"Where are you hurt?" asked Rosa, looking him over.

The man opened his bloodshot eyes and smiled.

Rosa smiled back.

He tried to sit, so Rosa helped him. His arm seemed to be stuck in one side of the blanket and he fought to free it. When he did, he withdrew a machete the size of Greg's and pushed Rosa onto her bottom. He raised the blade and gripped it with both hands to bring it down on her.

She screamed.

A second machete came from below to meet it, but the downward stroke knocked both blades into Rosa's shoulder. She fell backwards, her head bobbling onto the cracked ground. The dull clang of the metal next to her ear reverberated in her mind. Her shoulder and ribcage burned in pain and yet were oddly numb, but she didn't move, she just stared at the sky, the metallic clang resounding, not wondering about much besides the grey clouds and how they looked like they held rain. Blessed rain.

"Rosa, look at me. Rosa?"

Greg was standing over her. She couldn't focus on him. The blow to her body felt as though it had gone right through her. Greg fumbled with her clothes and she felt cold water drench her shoulder. She gasped. He helped her to sit.

"It'll hurt," said Greg, "but you'll be bruised more than you were cut. When we get back to the car, I'll put some antiseptic on it, but we need to move, now."

Rosa stared at him, dazed. She cocked her head to the side. "I've never noticed your eyelashes before," she said. "You have really nice eyelashes. Long. Wish I had long eyelashes."

"We need to go, now." Greg hauled her over his

shoulder with a grunt and ran.

Rosa retched from the pain. She looked behind them, suddenly bounced into awareness, but was sorry she had. Three men raced after them, all holding knives as long as swords. She prayed none carried a gun.

Greg shoved her into the driver's side door and she crawled over to the passenger seat as he barged in behind her. He already had the car running. They fishtailed, going nowhere for harrowing seconds before racing away. Her door flew open. She hung on and pull it closed, tears running down her face from the effort and the pain that shot through her shoulder.

They slowed down when Greg was certain they weren't being followed. "Put the antiseptic on your shoulder," he said. "Are you able?"

"I think so." Rosa flipped down the sun visor's vanity mirror. Her shirt was torn and her breast exposed. She covered it quickly, her cheeks red, but Greg was looking at the road, his face grim.

She extracted a singlet from her bag and turned away from Greg as best she could to inspect herself and change. Her shoulder was red around the wound though the cut was not deep, but it could turn septic, so she dabbed on the eucalyptus oil. She winced at the sting, though she felt better once she was dressed again.

"What were you thinking?" asked Greg in a quiet,

dangerous voice.

Rosa struggled to gather her thoughts. What *had* she been thinking? "I thought someone was injured and needed help."

"The world's not like that anymore!" said Greg. Rosa had never heard him so angry before. "You can't just be a Good Samaritan, you'll get killed."

"The whole reason I'm coming out here is to help as many people as I can," said Rosa, trying to get angry but instead sounding hurt. "How could I not check on someone laying on the side of the road?"

"Why didn't you get me when you heard him cry out? You were tricked by a small group that lure people with the crying ruse. They're pitiful. I woke to find you gone, Rosa. Do you know what that felt like? And then I was almost too late."

"You weren't."

"I might still be if you don't look after yourself." He paused, searching for something in the distance. When he spoke again, he was subdued. "Joy always went out first in the morning. She loved the sunrise, said it was the one thing that hadn't changed since the Rise. If she could wake up and see the sunrise, she would know everything was all right with the world. Except one morning, it wasn't. One morning she got up and was killed. A gang just passing by. That's it."

Rosa didn't push him for the rest of the story, because she had heard it from others. Greg had found each member that had been present, and, well, they weren't around to confirm or deny what Greg had done to them. Which, Rosa supposed, was a confirmation.

"It's cruel," she said, "that another person could end someone's life just in passing."

The thrum of road noise pressed between Rosa and Greg. She fidgeted. "I still don't see why you agreed to come. You've made it clear that I'm a burden and that you don't feel as strongly as I do about helping everyone."

Greg slammed on the brakes. He grabbed her arm and turned her to face him.

Her heart thundered. She regretted her words, but she was too scared to say anything else and make it worse.

"How could you say that?" said Greg. "Why do you think I try to help you every time I see you? I cop a lot from you. You've never appreciated my help, never grown up enough to see past your own selfish dreams."

"I—"

"No, don't talk! How can I call you selfish when you dream of helping others? Because you don't even help your own family. You're supposed to look after your own first, Rosa, then reach out to others. If you don't, there's no community, there's no home. I hoped you'd see that on this trip, hoped you'd grow up when you saw what the world was like, but even after what just happened, you can't admit that maybe your way of thinking about the world isn't the right way."

Rosa stared at her hands. "Are you going to take me back?" Perhaps she would deserve it. Some of what Greg said was true—she didn't show much interest in others, but it wasn't because she wasn't interested, it was because she focused on what was helpful to her. Perhaps she *was* selfish.

"I should," said Greg. "I've had enough of this, and yet, I always return to you. I've gone along with your ideas, I've even committed myself to this trip regardless of the lack of information you've given me." Greg's fingers relaxed their grip on her arm and slid down to rest atop her hand. "Why do you think I come past Aire as often as I do?"

Rosa hadn't thought it was very often at all, but then she hadn't ever asked Greg about the logistics of his trade business. "You've never told me anything."

"I would have if you'd asked, but you've always got some project on your mind. Do you ever think about me when I'm gone?" Greg's ruddy cheekbones became darker.

"I never stop thinking about you," said Rosa

quietly.

"I come back for you, Birdie. I always come back for you."

Rosa looked down at Greg's hand on top of her own. Her face warmed. Greg lifted her chin, and she opened her mouth to say something, but he kissed her. She leaned into it and rued her painful arm that she couldn't manoeuvre into a better position, but then she realised she should be thinking of Greg, and concentrated on his warm lips.

He drew away from her and grinned. She smiled back, then frowned. "I hear running water."

Greg deflated but was by her side in a flash, helping her out of the car. They walked down a gentle slope together. Trees dotted either side of a river. Normal green gum trees. Their silvery bark shone bright, and long, tapered leaves swayed in the breeze, the soft yellow flowers cheering Rosa considerably. She grasped Greg's hand and smiled as she took in the sunlight sparkling on the river.

He squinted, searching for danger, then frowned when he saw her smiling. "What do you see?"

"A river of diamonds."

"Even after what happened by the road back there?"

"Especially after what happened by the road back

there," she said, "but even more because of what happened in the car just now." Rosa drew close to him. He put his arm carefully around her. They watched the glistening water, together.

CHAPTER FIVE: WILD DOGS

"It's down there," said Rosa, pointing across the seawater rippling in the breeze. They stood on a small rise in a desert of dirt, staring at the encroached ocean. The sight hypnotised Rosa. In the distance, the tops of the tallest buildings of what had once been the capital of their state were visible. Melbourne.

It wasn't her first glimpse of the capital on the journey, but it was the first she could indulge herself and stare at it all she wished. Brief glimpses past Greg's head through the car window didn't count.

"What? Let me see that." Greg snatched the map from Rosa. He groaned. "No. No, no, Birdie, we can't go down that way. I knew I should've looked at the map before we left."

"What do you mean we can't go that way?" She stepped in front of Greg. "We've come all this way, and you tell me we can't go that way? Why not?"

"See here and here," said Greg as he smoothed the map onto the bonnet of the car. "The water's risen that far, creating a new peninsula which you can only get to through the bottleneck with Warragul in the middle. It's defensible and land is valuable, even if there's nothing on it, and that makes Warragul and the peninsula beyond some of the most disputed land in the country. The Wild Dogs hold the town at the moment. Is this plant of yours worth our blood?"

"A little blood is worth it to help a lot of people," said Rosa, though her voice was small.

She sat on the bonnet and stared across the barren fields the way they had come. It was a desert. What used to be farmland held nothing but dirt anymore. The seawater had contaminated the soil.

"*All* our blood," said Greg. "A little risk might have been worth it if the odds weren't stacked against us like a road train in front of a bicycle. We're leaving, now. This was as close as I was taking you in that direction, anyway. I don't see how keeping the map from me was supposed to make you feel better. You only delayed the inevitable, and you know it."

"That's not—"

"You take to heart all these old stories and books, where everyone's a hero and everything works out, but there's a reason the hero stories are fiction."

Rosa slid off the car, the hot wind fanning her anger. "Did you ever read anything when you were growing up? Have you lived all your life without anyone to look up to, no heroes to aspire to? That's a pretty sad admission."

"Rosa—"

"No, you listen to me, now. No matter what I do, you see me as a little girl with no idea about the world, don't you? You said before we left you would have kept me there if you could have. If you weren't really going to help me, why did you let me go?"

Greg grabbed Rosa's arms, pinning them to her sides, and lifted her into the air. She glared down at him as he glared up at her. She fought the urge to poke her tongue out at him. If he thought she was childish, she wasn't going to do anything to encourage him.

Greg sighed and put Rosa down. He sat on the bonnet, his shoulders slumped, and tapped for her to sit next to him.

Rosa huffed. "Your buttons are scratching the car," she said. "Not that it matters. You may as well crawl all over it with your buttons and your zippers."

"Stop being so realistic," said Greg, "you're

scaring me."

Rosa laughed, but it didn't hide the angry tears. She wiped them away with the bottom of her singlet top. She wasn't used to the dusty heat. Aire was hot, but the canopy of leaves always brought some relief. She rested against the car.

"I'm going to regret this," said Greg, shaking his head at himself, "but here goes. You've never let the futility of anything stop you before. You salvage parts that may never get used. You try to fix cars that may never run again. What would you have done if you'd made it this far without me and didn't know what I just told you?"

Rosa looked sideways at Greg but there was no sarcasm, no hint of a smile. He wasn't teasing her. "I would have driven straight in and straight into whoever is down there. I won't ask what would have happened to me. If you're not willing to go in there, it won't be anything I want to think about."

Rosa walked into the dunes, kicking up orange sprays of sand. She heard Greg slide off the car and cringed at the scraping paint. She turned to face him but kept walking backwards.

"Can I have a minute?" she asked. "Or is some crazy dune-beast going to eat me?"

Greg waved her on. The scratches on her car

revealed the red paint underneath in streaks. It looked like the car was bleeding. She turned to stare at the shimmering horizon. Here she was, out in the world, and it was as perilous as everyone said. After little more than a day, the threats and disappointments were overwhelming. Yet, she didn't want to return. Not empty-handed. But what other choice did she have? The dark thoughts gathered in her head like the storm clouds that frequented Aire.

She rested her foot on one of the large rocks dotting the landscape and traced the ridges with her toes.

"Rosa, get back here!" Greg raced towards her.

A crack echoed in the barrenness. Then another. Little puffs of dust popped at her feet. Rosa frowned at Greg, who was almost upon her, alarm written on his face.

Another crack. Rosa's leg seared in pain and crumbled beneath her. Her head hit the ground. She blinked away stars to see someone tackling Greg and grappling with him to keep him down. She tried to crawl over to help, but hands grasped her and hauled her up. Her cheek and forehead stung from being scraped across the ground.

"Don't hurt her!" Greg's shout was muffled as his head was pressed into the sand.

"What's that?" said the man on top of him with

a grin.

"Get off him." Rosa struggled, but her shoulder seized, and the stars returned when she moved her head. She tasted dirt.

"Any reason me and Bloodhound here shouldn't do away with you two and take that pretty car of yours?" said the man grinding his knee into Greg's back.

"Good of you to ask instead of concussing us first," said Greg, turning his head sideways and spitting out sand. "Let me up."

"Ease him up, Chuck," said Bloodhound, still holding Rosa.

Greg rose to his feet, managing to look unfazed despite Bloodhound's gun pointed at him. "I want to speak to your boss, Ridgeback. I'm Greg Valley."

Chuck shook Greg. "That supposed to mean something to me?"

"Enough, Chuck," said Bloodhound. "Yeah, it means something. It means if you don't want the Wardens on top of us, we take them to Ridge. Go get the ute. No hooning."

Bloodhound's gun stayed trained on Greg while Chuck left to get their ride. "The Valley himself. This has turned into an interesting day after all."

Greg didn't even glance at Bloodhound or his gun before he bear-hugged Rosa, breaking Bloodhound's hold on her.

Rosa squeezed her eyes shut and held onto Greg, waiting for the gun to fire. She heard Bloodhound move.

"No funny business, Valley," said Bloodhound.

"Just take my lead, okay?" whispered Greg into Rosa's ear. "I do this for a living, dealing with these sorts of people. We're married and partners in the family trade business. You simply tinker on cars. Tinker, and that's all. We're settling down and this is our last trade deal before we make a family. And never forget that Ridge—the Dogs' boss—is a sociopath, no matter how charming he seems. It'll be okay. Trust me." He gave her another squeeze and let go.

Rosa tried to commit to memory everything he'd told her. Bloodhound eyed them with distrust. It looked like he had taken a machete to his hair. Some patches were long, some were stubble, with a few scars mixed in. He grabbed Rosa's elbow again.

A convoy of utes approached. Each bonnet was crudely painted with a dog baring its teeth, just like those she'd seen at Aire. Rosa's anxiety heightened. She forced herself to study the utes, to search for a weakness to exploit. Lifted suspensions made room for larger wheels, and throaty rumbles were a telltale sign of the exhaust having been removed from behind the headers and replaced with a straight pipe. It was all just flash to look, and sound, intimidating. A surge of anger replaced some of her fear. These were the Dogs. They had attacked her home and countless other people's homes.

"You can drive, Missy," said Bloodhound, "but we'll be all around you."

"Greg stays with me," said Rosa with as much certainty as she could muster while being manhandled.

"Greg'll be riding with us," said Bloodhound. "Follow me, Missy. No mucking around, and I know the famous Greg Valley can read the odds and not do anything stupid himself. We're about twenty minutes out. Follow on."

Rosa got in her car, grasping the wheel to still her shaking hands. Chuck sat beside her. They took off, and she followed Bloodhound's ute, boxed in by three other vehicles. Their convoy kicked up a dust storm.

Rosa wished Greg was there to tell her what to expect. She didn't trust any of them—what if they did something to Greg? In her estimation, there was already too much violence and hostility for his trade gambit to work. She didn't even know what they were trading, so how was she supposed to play along? Her leg ached in agreement and made working the clutch difficult. Chuck's sniggers didn't help her nerves.

The desert gave way to old farms, the wire fences visible in patches where they hadn't been torn up or twisted into the ground. They followed a once-paved road that was rutted at best and churned up into chunks of tarmac at its worst. Rosa felt every bump thanks to her car's hard suspension. She suspected whatever terrain the car had rallied on hadn't been as treacherous as this.

They passed into the town, Rosa stunned by row upon row of abandoned houses.

"Never been to a large settlement?" asked Chuck. "Only trade with bog creek slums, do you?"

Rosa dug her fingernails into the steering wheel's stitching. "Just wondering at so few people," she said. "Did you drive them all out?"

Chuck snorted in answer.

Not for the first time, Rosa wondered at how much had been left behind. So much had happened over the years. The initial confusing exodus from people's homes, the resultant looting and destruction in the times of terror, different factions rising and falling, governments attempting to regain control but the population pushing back and creating new settlements, and the final abandonment of what people had once called home. The residents who were old enough to have experienced it, or those who salvaged outside of Aire, talked about how bad the rest of the country had it. Clive, the salvagers, Greg, all told the stories, but she had never really understood how bad it was until now.

The figure staring out of a broken window nearly made Rosa skid to a halt in shock. Someone had placed a life-sized figure of a pink bunny with a purple-spotted bowtie in the window. The wide smile was painted red, and the eyes seemed to follow her as she drove by.

The second one, a few houses later, was a giant mouse with a white-gloved hand waving at her. There were countless more, all cartoon anthropomorphic figures, each smiling, many waving. She would have enjoyed the spectacle if she hadn't been driving into a nightmare. Instead, her inability to fathom their meaning disturbed her.

They pulled into a large compound protected by high fences, topped with barbed wire and strung with animal skulls. Dogs. The gates slid shut behind them. The sign on the warehouse had once said *Bunnings*, though now only the adhesive could be seen, spelling out phantom letters.

Rosa parked where Chuck indicated. The other utes in the lot were identical to the ones in the convoy— as if they'd raided a showroom of new cars. The oddity increased her unease. She stepped out of the car and was pushed towards the warehouse. Greg caught her eye. At least they were both still alive.

***

Rosa's body ached, but her head was worse. Her leg still throbbed, but she could put weight on it—perhaps the injury wasn't too bad after all. Given their situation, she felt it was important to take in their surroundings, though it took great effort. They were in a part of the warehouse sectioned off by tall steel racks. Plastic boxes lined the shelves, enclosing the space and lending it an unwelcome sterility. The plastics and steel exuded strong smells in the heat. The floor was concrete, though her boots stuck to the rubber matting thrown on top.

Enough decent components to make at least four generators sat in a corner as scrap. Rosa shook her head at the waste and felt dizzy. Two head knocks in two days wasn't helping to keep a clear mind.

An entourage of five people walked through a gap between the racking. The central figure was shorter than most of the other men in the room, but his hair was neat and his beard trimmed, unlike everyone else. He was obviously Ridgeback, and the others were his bodyguards. One of Ridgeback's eyes was white, as was the scar that went from his nose to his forehead. She wondered if he was partially blind, amazed he had not lost his eye completely from such an injury.

Greg grasped Rosa's hand and she squeezed it back, welcoming the warmth and strength. They *were* supposed to be married.

Bloodhound stepped forward. "Boss," he said, "this here's Greg Valley and his partner. They're here to trade. They even have a gift for you. It's in the lot as we speak."

"A trade," said Greg from beside Rosa. "I'm a trader, Ridge, I don't do gifts."

Heads turned towards Ridgeback, waiting for his reaction. Rosa felt out of her depth already. She shuffled her weight from one leg to the other to stop her injured leg from cramping.

Ridge grinned. "I like you already. Finally, I get to meet the legend, and I'd expect no less than a trade from you. Where's your stock? What else do you have?" His blue eye landed on Rosa. "Your partner?"

Rosa shivered and felt goosebumps creep along her bare arms.

Bloodhound cut Greg's answer off. "Nothing else with them, Boss."

"Thank you, Bloodhound. Let the adults talk now." Ridge flicked his hand at Bloodhound, who seemed disgruntled at being dismissed. He moved to the side of the room but did not leave.

"Rosa is not for sale," said Greg. "We have no stock with us, yet we do have something valuable to trade. Would you like to inspect the car? Its quality will attest to the rest of our trade."

Rosa belatedly realised they were talking about her car. She had spent too much time on it to give it up, but her anger was a shadow compared to the dread of somehow ending up as gang property.

"Everything is for sale," said Ridge. "We need women in the settlement, and Rosa would be worth a fortune in trade. Bloodhound, take Rosa over there," he pointed to the far corner of the room, "away from Mister Valley so we can talk without distraction."

Bloodhound started for her, but his next step took him straight into the barrel of Greg's shotgun. Within seconds, every man had a gun trained on Greg, some had two. Rosa was frozen to the spot.

"Rosa is not for sale," said Greg again, "and our welcome is less than acceptable. I'm not in the mood for any more disrespect. Rosa stays with me."

"What's so valuable you think I can't simply kill you and take it? Not the car, surely. It's already mine, seeing as I don't like my privacy disturbed. You weren't relieved of your weapons either—another sign of good faith on my part. Don't make me regret that."

Greg barely missed a beat, though Rosa couldn't concentrate, her mind playing out terrible scenarios of what life would be like with the Wild Dogs. "I don't think you understand," said Greg. "I am here to offer you a permanent trade partnership. Your privacy is the reason no offer's been made before, as you protect it so absolutely. That means Rosa and I are honoured guests here. You've already made a slight by injuring us, so you owe us. The car we will trade in kind, for another with a full tank of fuel."

Ridge smiled. Confusion rippled around the room. He indicated with a finger that everyone should put their guns down, which they did with murderous stares at Greg and Rosa. "The Valley in his full splendour," said Ridge, his smile widening and his arms opening in a grand gesture. "In haggling, at least. Perhaps I shouldn't be so quick to test The Valley in his other famous attributes." Ridge paused. "Am I correct in hearing that it wouldn't be you I'd be trading with?"

"This is, as they say, my swan song," said Greg, and he slid his gun back into the straps on his back. "I'm settling down and won't be coming out this way again."

"I'm sorry to hear it," said Ridge. "The world will be a much duller place to have lost you. How will you guarantee a regular trade source if you're not supplying it? And the crux, what do you want in return?"

"As long you can guarantee the safety of our traders and a more welcome reception than we received today, I give you my word they will come. As to what we want, we want land. A piece of land for the traders to set up shop on."

Metallic clicks echoed in the room.

Ridge bared his teeth before forcing a smile. "I shouldn't be surprised. Men such as yourself don't shy away from an uphill battle." He waggled his finger at Greg as if telling off a naughty child. "You've been watching closely, seen that we are exhausting our supplies of food and water faster than we can replenish them. It's true we take what we find wherever we find it, but we cannot guarantee it will be enough, or timely. This partnership could be crucial to our survival as a faction. Does that bother you? Ensuring the longevity of an organisation such ours? It mustn't, you are here, after all." Ridge chuckled and shook his head. "It really is Christmas. You bring me the two things I want and need most in the world. If I didn't know that by taking one I would never get the other, I'd have her, no matter who you are."

Greg's fingers flexed, ready to grab the shotgun. Rosa got ready to dive to the floor. Then her leg cramped, and she clenched her teeth to stop herself from reaching down. Her eyes watered.

"As long as everything stays between us," continued Ridge, "agreed. A ute with a full tank, and land for a trade partnership, with our protection."

The room relaxed as much as a room full of armed gang members could.

"So tell me," said Ridge conversationally, "where will you settle? I see no rings, Greg. Are you lying to me? Because if you are, all bets are off."

Rosa stared at Greg, waiting for his brilliant mind to tell his mouth to say something. The seconds ticked by, yet Greg remained silent.

"You don't need rings to be married," said Rosa, her voice high-pitched due to fright. She pasted a bright smile on her face to compensate. "Besides, in our line of business, anything real shiny will attract unwanted attention."

Ridge's attention turned to Rosa. His gaze tested her courage more than all the guns in the room pointed at her just minutes ago had.

"If I ever see you again," said Ridge, "and there are no rings, I'll make you both permanent members of this settlement. You, dove, would particularly be an asset, in so many ways."

Rosa blanched, resisting the urge to cover her body with her arms.

"One thing doesn't add up . . ."

Rosa squeezed Greg's hand so tight he dug his fingernail into her palm to make her let go. She wanted to get out of there.

"How come Bloodhound found you parked outside the town?" asked Ridge. "Why didn't you drive straight in? I don't believe the famous Greg Valley fears my little old reputation, especially not since you were coming to trade and understand the repercussions of such a deal . . . see where I've hit a snag?"

Rosa tried her hardest to blush. She looked at her toes and shuffled around a little, grasping Greg's hand to her chest. "That's my fault. It's embarrassing, but . . . I love the sea. We stopped because it was a perfectly lovely view of the water from there."

Silence. Then Ridge laughed. "You're a young thing to be taken by the sea, after all it has taken itself. Right then, I've got a solution. I've been told by an eager little bird on the way in that you tinker with cars and such. You do me a bit of a favour and see if you can mend my boat down by the bay, and if you do, you both can have the first cruise in it. Now, for me owing you, Bloodhound will show you to your room for the night. Best hotel in my territory."

Ridge turned to leave. "And with my charity, I crush my reputation as a tyrant." He said the last to himself, but Rosa was so giddy at the conversation being over, she giggled. Greg's painfully tight grip on her hand quelled that.

Bloodhound drove them to a nearby hotel where Ridge himself stayed. The building was in good repair compared with others in the Dogs' territory, and a lemon tree grew out the front. It was an old building with flourishes that reminded Rosa of the old ranches in comic books.

"I got to see you in action, Greg," said Bloodhound as they walked up the path, "and I'll remember it. Almost a pity I didn't see The Valley in all his glory, eh? Probably for the best, if the stories I've heard are true. Are you one of them, eh? Brings new meaning to 'The Valley' if you are . . ." Rosa frowned at Bloodhound as he stared at Greg expecting an answer. He shook his head when none came. "I'll be here at sun-up."

Rosa locked the door while Greg looked through the window to make sure Bloodhound left. As soon as it was clear, Greg enveloped Rosa in a hug. He spoke into her hair, "We've come away with our lives. Most are not so lucky when they meet Ridgeback." He kissed her on the forehead and she got prickles along her spine from his words. "We're not out of here yet though, so keep it up."

Rosa steadied herself in Greg's arms. It had been a long day. She forced herself to take a step back and ask her questions.

"Okay, Mister Famous Greg Valley, talk to me."

"We're alive," he said and sank onto the mattress. He rubbed his face before looking at her again. The stubble was already coming through on his chin and the shadow heightened his look of weariness.

"Thank you for that," she said. She sniffed the bed linen before sitting beside him. It smelled clean. "Though I've been shot in the leg."

Greg inspected her wound. "Just a bit of rock. Would you like me to amputate the leg now, or want to sleep on it and decide in the morning?"

Rosa walloped Greg in the shoulder.

He grinned. "Hang on a tick and I'll fix it up."

Greg rummaged around in his pack and returned with a small first-aid kit.

"I still don't understand how we're alive," said Rosa.

"I was lucky Bloodhound had heard of me," said Greg as he cleaned the wound. "I hoped the Wild Dogs might want to trade, and I was right. Visiting in my official capacity was the only thing we could do."

"But what exactly is that?" asked Rosa. "Bloodhound, Ridgeback . . . they looked impressed, Greg, and maybe a little afraid. I thought you traded with settlements? I knew you were a mercenary, but I assumed you were defending the merchandise against attacks. This seems like a whole lot more to me. What don't I know?"

"What you should be asking is how we're getting out of here unscathed," he said. "I'll make it easy. Just keep following our story. You did great today."

"I want to know what's going on," said Rosa. "Don't I deserve that?"

"For once in your life can you listen to me?" Greg tugged the bandage so hard the end tore off. Rosa flinched. "Sometimes you don't always get what you want when you want it or the way you want it. Sometimes you have to make the best of what you have."

"I listened to you today," said Rosa, scratching where her leg was already itching under the bandage. "I made a real effort. I understand we're still in trouble, and perhaps this is the wrong place to discuss whatever it is you do, but don't think I'm going to forget about this. Once we're out of here, you tell me. You owe it to me."

Greg nodded, sage once more.

"We have to be real careful here, Rosa," he said. "I'm getting a picture of what's happening with the Dogs, and it's not only Ridge we've got to watch out for. He lords over them and is brutal to open disobedience, but the way he dismissed Bloodhound and how the other Dogs seem to do whatever they want behind his back . . . If Ridge had the Dogs under his thumb that would be a different matter, but it will be a hard-sell to get anyone out here in this climate, and I can't come out here to help set it up."

"Oh, but I want to see The Valley in action."

Greg looked Rosa square in the eyes. "No, you don't. Pray that never happens."

CHAPTER SIX: REFLECTION

Rosa woke in a too-soft bed, a thin sheet tangled around her legs. Greg sat on the end of the bed watching her struggle to extricate herself. He had a package in his hands.

"What is it?" Rosa sat against the wall and positioned a pillow behind her back.

Greg opened the box and pulled out a long sundress patterned with tiny blue flowers.

"No," said Rosa.

"Agreed, but to keep the peace, please wear it. Ridge is trying to make a point, and if you don't, he'll no doubt say we owe him. He's making this a game. It wouldn't surprise me if the boat we're going to see doesn't exist, though I don't know what will be waiting for us if not."

"How about if *you* wear it?"

Greg threw the dress at Rosa and she went into the bathroom to change. When she stepped out, she saw a hint of a smile in Greg's eyes.

She looked down. The diamond neckline framed her cleavage, which had likely been the intention.

"At least it's long," said Greg. "He could have given you undies to wear. Only undies. Probably would have if he'd had any."

"Scratch that thought from your mind."

Greg grinned, dimples showing, and walked to the door. "Don't pay any mind to what you see outside. Don't ask, either, Bloodhound's out there."

Greg opened the door and stepped over something. Rosa lifted her long skirt so it didn't slide across the body at the door. Or the other two further out.

She didn't see Bloodhound anywhere, so she whispered, "Alive?"

Greg shot her a warning glance but nodded. Why had the men been sent to their room? How had she slept through whatever happened to them?

The wide-mouthed leer Bloodhound gave her made Rosa want to kick him. She still wore her boots, so if she aimed well he might regret his chuckle. She eyeballed Greg's machete, and Greg raised his eyebrows at her. She shrugged. "Wasn't going to do anything," she mumbled.

They rode in silence with the static of Bloodhound's prattle as background noise. He seemed a fan-boy of Greg's, and Rosa dismissed his chatter from her mind when she realised they were heading to the bay. Her bay. Her desalination plant.

***

The tide ebbed a fraction before Rosa's toes. The road she stood on continued into the water. Seeing the white lines disappear, and the partially submerged buildings rise like hands asking for help, awakened a deep sorrow and made the destruction of thirty years past real for her. What had it been like, living through the Rise?

She studied her map. The waters had risen far more than she had expected. They were kilometres from the Wonthaggi township, let alone the plant, and the buildings she saw were the tops of farmhouses. The plant was unreachable. Completely consumed.

"You still keen, Birdie?" asked Greg from behind her. He hadn't bothered to watch her fix the boat, opting to stand guard several metres away. "We don't need to test the darn thing. It'd be best to leave Dog territory behind quickly."

"I am." Rosa wouldn't let the chance go, not when she was so close. She filled the boat with the fuel provided by Ridgeback. The fix had been simple—too simple—but she couldn't fathom a motive behind it. "You coming?"

Greg slowly made his way over. Rosa waved for him to hurry. They pushed the boat out together. Her mind was on the map and navigating around the buildings.

Once Greg settled, Rosa started the engine and spared a glance at Bloodhound who had fallen asleep in the back of his ute some way off. He had shed his shirt and rolled his pants halfway up his calves to keep cool. He didn't even stir at the noise from the boat.

"Don't dismiss him so easily," said Greg, noticing her gaze. "He's the one the men listen to, not Ridge."

Rosa frowned at Greg.

"You've visibly relaxed," he said, "and I don't think it was fixing the boat that did it. It's Bloodhound. His constant flattering of me is drawing you off-guard. Don't let it. I don't believe those men came in the night without him knowing. He was testing me, and if I'd failed, he wouldn't have hesitated to come for you."

"Okay, I get it."

"I mean it, Rosella. I can hear your scepticism. He's making a show of being out here alone with us.

Consider how highly he thinks of me, he's no doubt told everyone else, and they will see him return unharmed. I'm not blowing my own horn, but he is blowing his, and it's a ten-foot air-horn."

"Okay," said Rosa, squeezing Greg's leg and looking him straight in the eyes. "I'll mind him."

Rosa guided them out, albeit unsteadily. Even going slow, piloting the craft was difficult. It was a pleasant, non-threatening day if she didn't think about Greg's warning and Bloodhound waiting for them back at shore. The sky held no storm clouds, though Rosa wished Joe the weather-reader was with them to confirm.

The water was clear enough to follow the roads at the bottom. There wasn't as much debris as she expected, either. She still felt the tiniest amount of apprehension at the water spraying in a mist over her face, especially considering the plants they had seen on their trip so far, but she hoped any water toxicity would be minimal considering the time elapsed since the Rise.

Strange, motionless white blades pierced the otherwise smooth waterscape at intervals. Rosa steered close to one. It loomed over the boat.

"What are they?" she asked Greg. "Windmills?"

"Wind *turbines*," he said. "Thought you would've asked me about them yesterday when we passed the wind farm."

She peered down into the water, seeing the base of the structure extend below her. She *had* seen turbines towering in the distance yesterday. Remembering them changed her perspective on the depth of the water. She felt queasy. Could the blades still move partially submerged? She gave the remainder a wide-berth, just in case.

Greg fell unusually silent. She glanced over at him and noticed that the colour had gone from his face. The sun shone on a sheen of sweat on his forehead. His hand was white-knuckled on the edge of the boat, and below his rolled-up sleeves, the veins on his forearms protruded. He stared at the bottom of the boat doggedly.

Rosa was on sudden alert. "Greg, what is it?" She shut off the engine. She felt his head and took his wrist. He was clammy and his pulse was racing. "What's wrong? Do you want to lie down?"

Greg ran his fingers through his hair and tugged at his roots.

Rosa took his hands into hers and rubbed them in what she hoped was a comforting way. "Tell me," she said. "Please."

Greg exhaled roughly. He shook his head, then nodded. "I should have told you," he said quietly.

"Told me what?" said Rosa, coaxingly. She smoothed down his scruffy hair with one hand.

"I've never come back to the sea since the Rise. My family . . . we were caught in it. I was twelve."

Rosa leaned forward and rested her head against his for a moment. He had been *twelve*. "Concentrate on slowing your breathing," she said, sitting up again and stroking his cheek. "Make sure you don't inhale more than you exhale or else you'll feel worse."

Greg's face scrunched in concentration, which probably meant he wasn't succeeding.

"We're going back." Rosa moved towards the engine.

"No," said Greg, pulling her away from the engine. "They can't see me like this."

Rosa sighed inwardly. She was trying to help. "Okay, we'll wait a minute, see if you feel better. If not, we'll think of something. I'm sure you'll be fine once we get back to land." Rosa felt far from confident, but if Greg was out of action, she was in charge and had to act like it.

Greg shook his head with tiny movements. "Crook over a puddle of water."

Rosa looked into the depths below them. Massive pipes far below them curled into a labyrinth. The beginnings of her desalination plant. She rested her chin on the edge of the boat. The Rise had created a whole other world. New plants had attached themselves to the ruined piping. Steel and concrete structures had become artificial reefs, and creatures swam about on their business, not knowing it wasn't originally their world.

Tiny octopuses stuck to the side of the boat, slowly making their way up and around, inspecting the craft. Rosa craned over. From far away they seemed to glide, but up close, their movements were tremulous and clumsy. They were, however, almost cute. They varied in size, but some were as small as peas, and Rosa watched them gather, mesmerised.

"What are you looking at?" asked Greg. "Don't make me jump in after you if you fall overboard. Really, really don't." He sounded like he had regained some of his humour.

"They've made it their home." She felt a pang of longing for what lay beneath. For months she had dreamt about the filters. Now she was the closest she would ever be. "Are you good to go yet?"

"Give me a tick."

Rosa watched a large octopus making its way through the water. It was an amazing creature, yet as it got closer—ridiculously fast—she saw it was larger than their large boat, and coming straight for them.

Suddenly the cute, teeny octopuses were menacing little scouts for their captain. Rosa remembered what Greg had said about the ladybirds not being all they seemed. She flicked some of the little imps off the boat, though whatever miniature waves of information they had been sending had already been received. The captain was upon them.

"Moment's over." Rosa grabbed Greg's machete and swung at the first arm grasping the boat. She hit true, and the severed part fell into the boat twitching and spraying blue blood.

Rosa gunned the motor. It fizzled.

Another arm snaked over the side, and Rosa kicked it, cringing as her boot sank into the hard rubber of the arm more than expected. It withdrew into the water.

Greg clambered over to her. When he was within reach, she pushed him back down with her foot. "Don't move." She gunned the motor a second time.

It said something about Greg's condition that he wasn't fighting her to get a look.

Where was the captain? She looked over the side in time to see it flinging itself back at them. Before Rosa could duck or brandish the machete again, the octopus was climbing into the boat. An arm snaked around Rosa and she heard Greg groan as the boat rocked violently. "You're going to make me get up, aren't you?" he said.

She tried to prise the arm off, but a spray of ink covered her arm and her fingers slipped. The boat lurched again, and Rosa fell, grabbing at the exposed planks of the hull to keep from being pulled overboard.

"Stay down," said Greg. He trained his shotgun on one of the arms and fired. The bottom of the boat splashed blue. Instead of letting go, the octopus pulled. Rosa thought her legs were going to come off. Then the arms slid off all at once and the octopus was gone with an almighty splash.

Rosa forced herself up and grabbed the machete. She looked over the side. An even bigger octopus—dwarfing the twenty-foot captain that had tried to capsize their boat—pulled the first octopus into its horrendous beak.

With a strangled cry, Rosa revved the motor and got out of there. The strength of the creatures was awesome—and terrifying. She hoped that the giant wasn't following the boat now, reaching its long tentacles out in a crushing grasp.

When they were almost back to shore, Rosa started laughing, her mind's way of releasing the pent-up stress, fear, and disappointment. "I've got the perfect excuse for your condition now," she said, "and the severed arm is our proof." She continued to laugh, even as she roughly landed the boat, and even as she knew her hopes and plans for the world had drowned.

***

"Another legend to see The Valley into retirement," said Ridgeback, holding the octopus arm away from him. "I'd keep it as a trophy, but it already stinks. Bloodhound informed me the boat is fixed, if a little inked. Your ute's all set to go, one of our Rangers, but before you leave, I have a final request."

Greg stiffened beside Rosa. Outwardly, he seemed to have made a complete recovery from their time in the boat.

"Rosa, dove, would you show me what's so special about that lovely car of yours?"

Rosa glanced at Greg, but he didn't indicate a course of action either way. She didn't see how she could refuse. "Of course."

"Mister Valley, it has been a pleasure." Ridge inclined his head. "Bloodhound will show you to the Ranger. Rosa will be along shortly."

Greg scowled and squeezed Rosa's hand, hard, before he left.

Rosa followed Ridge, furiously thinking about what she was supposed to show him. They walked into the parking lot, but she couldn't see her car anywhere. They continued across the lot to a second warehouse. Rosa's steps faltered. What was she getting herself into?

"I've shifted that beaut of yours away from prying eyes," said Ridge, unlocking the door. He held it open for her. "Take a look. You'll like what you see."

She shouldn't go in there with him. There was no way she could justify such stupidity to herself or Greg. But what else could she do? She walked a few steps towards the warehouse to see inside the door, and to give herself another moment to think.

What was inside made her gasp and jog the last few steps into the warehouse. Out of the corner of her eye, she saw Ridge grin. Every square foot of the warehouse was filled with cars—cars in near-mint condition. Her WRX was in the pride of place before her, already sanded down and ready to paint. She walked towards it as if in a dream and ran her hands over the bodywork.

"What colour should she be?" asked Ridge from beside her.

Reminded of the predicament she had stepped into, her eyes darted to the door. Closed, and no doubt locked. Rosa looked back at the car. She had underestimated Ridge. He had set the lure, and she had taken the bait. Well, she had only come up with one plan, so she would stick with it—stall. Stall until another opportunity presented itself.

"That dress is definitely becoming on you," said Ridge, looking her over. "Even covered in grease, ink and octopus blood, you're lovely. Perhaps blue for the car, to match?" He gave her the keys. "Work your magic."

Rosa frowned. "What do you want me to do?"

"Such a loaded question." His grin made her shiver. "Just check the engine, whatever you usually do."

Rosa took a deep, shaky breath, then set to work with the tools Ridge had set out for her. Everything would be all right. She would get out of there . . . somehow. She quickly disconnected the air compressor system from the car. It was too awkward to take with her, so she had to trust her instinct that no-one in the gang would realise what it was and see how adept she was at modifying vehicles. Greg's warnings had finally sunk in, causing paranoia.

She felt Ridge's hot breath on the back of her neck. She turned around so fast the tools clattered to the ground.

"Are you absolutely sure you won't reconsider joining us?" he asked. "Watching you work was . . . astounding . . . as I knew it would be after you fixed the boat, and I feel like I may have been cheated after all." He brushed along her shoulder and arm with the back of his hand, admiring the goosebumps it created.

"All right there, Rosa?" Greg's voice broke Ridge's uncomfortable gaze. "Finished showing Ridgeback everything he needs to know?"

The startled look on Ridge's face told Rosa he

must have locked the door. Thank goodness for Greg's undisclosed talents.

"Yes, all done." She handed the keys back to Ridge.

"I don't think I've met a more fascinating couple," said Ridge. "Remember what I said to you? If I see you again without rings, all bets are off?"

"Rosa, get here now." Greg moved towards her, but Ridge was too close and slid his arm around her neck and dragged her backwards. Rosa dug her nails into Ridge's arms. He squeezed tighter.

Greg aimed his shotgun, but Ridge shielded his body with Rosa.

"You know what he is, dove?" Ridge whispered. "Who would you prefer? The man who is upfront about the monster he is, or the one who hides in the shadows?"

Rosa tried to elbow Ridge, but he squeezed tighter and she felt dizzy from the lack of air. Then she heard a click behind her.

"Let the girl go," said a deep voice. Bloodhound.

Ridge finally relinquished his hold on Rosa, and she stumbled towards Greg, gasping. Greg pulled Rosa close, nodding to Bloodhound who had his gun pressed into Ridge's neck. Greg moved his arm so Rosa couldn't see them anymore and helped her away. Once they were outside, she heard a single shot.

Greg led her to one of the snarling dog utes and drove them out of there. The gate to the compound was open, but Rosa didn't question it.

He stopped as soon as they were out of the Dogs' territory. "Check the car. Make sure we're not driving a bomb."

Rosa hopped out and immediately knelt in the sand and threw up. A man was dead. She had almost become the Dogs' breeder. Or tortured. Or dead. She threw up again. When she'd stopped heaving, Rosa stood and kicked sand over everything. She returned to the car and found a spare set of clothes to change out of the dress. Ridge's dress. A cold shiver prickled along her arms and down her back. When she had changed, Greg helped her dig a shallow hole to bury the dress in.

She checked the car over as thoroughly as possible on the side of the road. Usually, it would calm her, but what she found increased her discomfit.

She popped her head in Greg's open window. "Take a look at the battery. I—I think it's a *new* battery."

That got Greg moving. He inspected the battery and whistled at what he found. He pointed to a small symbol on the side, a blue map of pre-Rise Australia with white stars circling the inside. "That's a gov-state symbol. And you reckon the battery looks new? See that symbol anywhere else?"

They poked around the engine bay for more symbols. Rosa couldn't see anything else suspicious, but they didn't have enough time to go over the ute meticulously.

Greg grabbed their blanket from the back seat and smoothed it over the bonnet, tucking it in before shutting it. "We just hit the jackpot in trade-able info, Birdie. It confirms my suspicions over something the gov-state's been trying to hush up. I think whatever little gov is left might have access to resources no-one knows about. The world might just be making amends, but if only a select few know about it, they can keep the population in check. The implications are endless."

"Would now be a good time to mention I saw boxes with those symbols in the warehouse? I didn't know what they were, then."

Greg rubbed his eyebrow. "The best scenario for everyone would be that the Dogs stole a shipment. They might not even realise what they have—if they did, I doubt they would have given us this vehicle. Is it safe to drive?"

"I didn't find anything major," said Rosa, as she hopped into the car. Greg took off straight away. "Though it needs tyres, like everything." She was quiet for a moment. "He's not alive anymore, is he?"

"Ridge? He was not an okay bloke," said Greg.

"He was a crook, so don't go wasting any grief over him. What did he say to you when you were alone?"

"He . . . he asked if I knew who you really were," she said, inspecting the glove box. Rosa was surprised by how clean everything was. She hadn't expected the Dogs to have taken such good care of their cars. "I know he was only trying to put me off-balance. There's more to you than what I've seen, I know that. Everyone has their secrets."

Greg gave her a searching look.

"He said we cheated him. After watching me work on my car."

"Work on?" said Greg. "You were only meant to show it to him."

"Anything I would have done in front of Ridge would have looked spectacular. He's not—wasn't— mechanically minded. He couldn't fix the boat when only a few components were loose, though even my fixing that wowed him. And in their warehouse was a pile of generators. I could have fixed them and we would have had at least four, yet they just left them sitting there like pieces of junk."

Greg squeezed Rosa's thigh in reassurance. "Ridge wanted you right from the beginning. After he saw what you could do, he used it as an excuse to renege on his trade deal. You know that Bloodhound offered me a position with them when he was showing me the ute? It makes sense why he let us out in the boat alone, now. He wanted to show he trusted me."

Rosa turned to stare at Greg. What was it about him that attracted everyone? There was so much she didn't know about him, but for her, it was his loyalty. He was steadfast to those he loved.

"I declined, naturally," he continued. "He really wanted to ensure the trade deal would transfer to him. Everything we agreed with Ridge would remain the valid terms, but he also gave me his word Ridge would get what's coming to him. When Ridge went after you, seems it sped up Bloodhound's endeavour. It's best to be far away from here."

Rosa watched the drought-stricken landscape change into a waterlogged marsh. She looked at it with new eyes, more fully realising the effects of the Rise on the country. In Aire, they frequently weathered terrible storms and torrential rain, but she had grown up with that terrifying norm. They lost people in the storms, but it was a part of life. Now she saw firsthand how good Aire was compared to everywhere else. She had only travelled across one state, but it felt like a different world. A world in which she was lost.

"Greg," said Rosa, "why don't we find somewhere to settle? You and me. We could make our own home somewhere."

"That's a beautiful sentiment," said Greg, not hearing—or choosing to ignore—the desperation in Rosa's voice, "but to get where Aire has gotten takes a lot of work and heart and perseverance and luck. It would take decades. I know you don't want to go back empty-handed, but sometimes that's what happens."

"All I ever wanted was to help others. To be out in the world, like you. I understand how precious Aire is now, but I need to be free."

"You're free to choose whatever you want, Birdie, but would it be so bad to live there?"

Rosa watched the insects buzz above the marsh. The wind blew a rotten smell towards them that hadn't been there on the way out.

"Take me to your majestic pub," she said. "What was it, the Bore?"

Greg hit the brakes. Rosa glared at him as she rubbed her chest where the seatbelt dug into her wound. At least the pre-tensioner still worked.

"Why in this flooded land do you want to go there?"

Rosa shrugged.

"Oh no," he said, "you have to answer. It's a fair hike from here, we'd have to kip in the car again because we wouldn't make it before dark. Why would you think I would take you there? If you want a drink, here." He passed her his flask.

"You can keep that petrol knock-off to yourself. I want you to take me out and buy me a decent drink before I decide whether or not to return home . . . And maybe we could find out about other desal plants?"

"Trade information, Birdie, trade." He tapped a finger on the steering wheel, considering. "You want me to take you on a date to an infamous pub in the middle of a country that feuds over water and land, after just meeting one of the worst guerrilla gangs and dealing in black-market trade with them, almost becoming Ridgeback's woman, seeing a bloody rise to new leadership, and at said pub, you want to betray the gang and the government's secrets for your own gain?"

Rosa held her breath for so long she could feel it beating at her lungs.

"Okay," said Greg. "I could use a drink."

CHAPTER SEVEN: TRIBUTE

Greg parked out the front of a two-storey building in a town called Beechworth. The pub resembled the old hotels Rosa had seen in tourist pamphlets in glove-boxes. She could only make out 'Well' on the old sign overhead. The rest had faded into oblivion, as with most things in the country.

The number of cars out the front suggested no-one had any qualms about liquor before lunchtime. Rosa eyeballed the Navara they parked beside. It was modified to run truck wheels, like the Dogs', though these were even larger. She could easily see through the gap between wheel and fender. The other ute nearby was a nondescript piece of metal with no windscreen or doors.

Its air box jutted out of a butchered bonnet, and thick bars were bolted across the roof and over the door frames in a makeshift roll cage. Small skulls of various animals were zip-tied onto the roll bar. What was it with people and skeleton adornments?

Greg placed his hands on her shoulders. "These guys are a shady lot. They will twist your words like you wouldn't believe. Their job is talk, and they thrive on secrets, so even something as seemingly innocent as where you're from or where you've been can be used against you. Try to keep quiet. Please."

Rosa felt a twinge of anxiety at what they were planning to do. This was her last chance to make her plans—and her father's dreams—a reality.

The Well was pretty impressive, though it appeared that only repeated repairs—and the combined will of everyone wanting a pub—kept it standing. It all added to the charm. Various nooks and booths sat around a central bar area. The rafters and stair railings were strung with multicolour string lights, and—intermittent missing LED's notwithstanding—it was a festive touch Rosa appreciated.

Smiles and shouts of greeting welcomed Greg, but also surreptitious glances from dark corners. On the whole, most of the faces seemed friendly, and Greg even got a few pats on the back and offers of drinks.

Greg held Rosa's hand as they walked to the bar. He was taking the date thing to heart. Either that, or he was worried about the other patrons. The sheer amount of weaponry in the room—on backs and hips and tables—was alarming.

"When you arrive at The Well," said Greg, "you see Larry first."

The man behind the bar was slightly cleaner than most of the patrons, though his apron was caked with grime. "Greg, it's been an age. I figured you must've died," he said matter-of-factly. It probably did happen a lot.

"Larry, how are you, mate?" said Greg. "Nah, I'm still kicking. Brought a date, in fact. This is Rosa."

"Well hello, lovely lady." Larry dipped his head. "Greg's a mighty fine man to have. I wish you both long lives. What'll it be?"

"Two scotches," said Greg.

"Right up."

Greg sat on a barstool and Rosa took the one beside him.

Larry placed two glasses in front of them. "Them's free from what's owed. Now we're square."

Greg nodded his thanks. "Any news, Larry? Heard anything about Mack?"

"Always news, nothing you'd be interested in

though. Mack ain't been seen near as long as you." Larry polished the countertop with his grimy apron. "If I remember right, he drank like a hound was on his heels, but that's nothing new. Come to think of it, when he left he said he was going north, but three people told it he went west." He shrugged before moving on to serve the next patron.

Greg closed his eyes for a moment, the only outward sign of his troubled thoughts about Mack. Then he lifted his glass to Rosa. They clinked. "Cheers."

Rosa sniffed the drink first, then took a tentative sip. It wasn't petrol. It wasn't horrible. She tried to enjoy it while taking everything in. The pub was like a library for street signs, Australiana, and, oddly, plants. Wherever the sunlight came through a gap, a pot plant rested, or a jar enclosed with some cactus. They were saving the world in their own, small way. Behind the bar hung a board with embroidered symbols, like patches on jackets, pinned to it.

"Noticeboard," said Greg, following her gaze. "Symbols are mercs that have jobs need doing, those on the bottom right are those for hire."

"Are you up there?" asked Rosa.

"Not in an age," said Greg. "Just relax. Stick to the plan and don't give too many details."

Rosa flushed hot. Perhaps it was just the effect of

the alcohol, but she still had half her drink to go.

"Drink it slow," said Greg, a hint of amusement in his voice. "Tribute is a salute to pre-Rise alcohol, and she's strong. Come on." Greg took her hand again. "I'll give you the tour."

She followed Greg to the middle of the lower level and he waved his hand to indicate the entire place. "This is The Well. Stay away from upstairs, that's where the bad element lingers."

In the intermittent shadows of the string lights, Rosa could see tables on the overhanging balcony. "You can gamble away your livelihood up there," he said. "Anything can be used to buy-in, as long as it's worth enough to the person offering it. I once saw a man buy-in with a lilly pilly tree, another with a ginger cat. That's the tamest it gets, however." He lowered his voice. "Remember what I told you before we came in? The real trades are in secrets. Information."

"Greg! Oi, Greg, come over here."

They joined a table with two men and a woman. The woman's long hair was shaved off over one ear, but the length was braided in a delicate design, like a daisy amongst thorns. She wore a lot of hard leather like most of the people in the room. Rosa glanced at the men. They were of a similar age to Greg, though one was missing half his cheek to a vicious scar, and the other man's only distinguishing feature was a severe jawline made more prominent by large sideburns.

"Who's your friend, Greg?" asked the woman. "She looks far too young to partner with you. If I'd known you'd been looking . . ." The woman lifted her bottle, slowly moving it past her chest, to take a sip.

"Then I suppose it's lucky you didn't know, Flic," said Greg.

Rosa couldn't help but grin as Flic's face fell. All three of the men laughed.

Greg pointed to Scarface. "This is Johno." And then to Sideburns. "And Dennison. Denny."

Rosa gave a small wave.

"Really though, who is the lovely lass?" asked Johno, with a crooked grin. His voice was gravelly, but he spoke with an endearing lisp because of his disfigurement.

"This is Rosa."

All three stared at him for more information. Even Rosa stared, waiting for his explanation. Greg looked slightly put out, but Rosa couldn't help him. Were they still pretending to be married?

After the silence stretched too far, Rosa filled the gap. "I'm his mechanic."

Eyebrows shot up.

"You always hold hands with your mechanic,

Johno?" Denny asked.

"I would if they were as darling as this one." Johno placed his hand on top of Rosa's and winked.

Rosa grinned.

"Don't you sweet talk her," said Greg, "and don't you let him charm you, Rosa. He's a royal bastard, this one."

They all laughed, though Rosa was on the outside of the joke so she just smiled.

"Where d'you find her, Greg?" Flic still looked at Rosa as if she were a dirty dog come into a clean room. "She really is fresh."

"Lay off, Flic. She's a tough nut. She took a bullet to the leg yesterday and barely said a word about it." Greg winked at Rosa before continuing. "What have you all been up to? Any news I should hear?"

Rosa kept an ear on their conversation as she listened in to others. She heard snippets, but nothing worth paying attention to. She rolled the glass against her cheek in a futile effort to cool down. With so many people inside, the air was stifling, and her head swirled.

A musician strummed a guitar in a dim corner. All Rosa could see were fingers bedazzled with coloured plastic jewels. Rosa supposed showing any real jewels of that size would have ended badly. It was difficult to hear the guitar over the buzz of voices, but what she heard was well-played. She began to enjoy herself.

"Had a bad trade not long ago," Denny was saying. He dragged his chair closer to Greg's. "Up north at one of them gov facilities. Not much to be said except they relieved us of our wares, and me and one other bloke were the only ones who made it away. They're getting nastier, I tell you. Best to stay out of their whole state. What about you, mate?" he asked Greg. "Any news?"

Greg swirled the last of his drink around before downing it. "Actually, think it's about time I hang up the boots. Thought I'd stop by and say my goodbyes."

Denny stared at Greg as if his idol had died.

"If I had a mechanic like your lass," said Johno with a nod of his head at Rosa, "I'd be doing the same. We can only wish you a quiet life from now on."

Denny couldn't find any words, so he lifted his bottle in a toast to Greg. Rosa lifted her glass, feeling no words were adequate either. What did Greg mean? He'd said the same thing to the Wild Dogs, though she had assumed he was just talking his way out of there. Was he serious? He had also been talking about spending time in Aire . . . Perhaps that's why he had obliged to take her on this trip in the first place—a final goodbye. Her stomach felt like it had hit the floor.

"Also," Greg continued, "I have a final prop for you. I've set up a trade opening with the Wild Dogs."

Johno snorted, then coughed as beer went up his nose. Denny paled, his hand shaking around his raised bottle. Flic tapped her fingernails on her bottleneck as if trying to pierce the glass.

Greg seemed to be tying up loose ends. Was Rosa the next one?

"Good one, mate." Johno wiped the tears from his eyes.

"He's serious," said Denny. He hadn't taken his eyes off Greg. "I didn't believe you about retiring, not until you said that."

Johno studied Greg's face. "Ah, hell, Greg, what a way to go out. You're either going to be credited with the biggest trade agreement in history, or get us all killed. Either way, you'll have legend status forever now."

Flic noisily scraped her chair as she left to get another drink. There was a lull in the conversation where Greg fidgeted in a way Rosa knew meant he was getting ready to leave.

Johno must have noticed too because he came around to Greg's side. "Mind if I have a word?" he asked.

Greg hesitated a second. "Rosa? Denny? Don't talk each other into any mischief."

Rosa scowled at Greg as he walked a little way off with Johno. It was now or never.

"Hey, Denny," she said, trying to sound

nonchalant, "you get around. Know of any desalination plants not completely underwater?"

A hush descended around their table. Faces turned towards her, and she realised she had been speaking louder than she intended. She scowled at her empty glass. A buzz of whispers circled the room, and the heads of those who couldn't have heard turned her way as well. Even the musician's fingers froze on the strings like startled spiders. Rosa's skin crawled.

Greg appeared behind her, grasped her shoulder and laughed. "She's only mucking around, lads. Early April Fool's joke. As you were."

"That's not something to be taken lightly," said Johno, coming up behind them as conversation slowly returned to the room. "Especially not when you just blow in here after an age."

Flic sat across from them with her fresh drink. "You caught unwanted attention, no doubt about it." She smirked.

Rosa scowled. How could any of them stand being around Flic for more than ten minutes?

"Is that what you meant by retirement, mate?" asked Denny, his face flushed. "You shacking in with those pricks now? I wouldn't have thought you for gov, mate, it breaks the spell. Tell us it isn't true."

"It isn't true," said Greg, deadpan.

"Seems an awful coincidence," said Johno. "Though you aren't as stupid as all that to announce it, so maybe the lass really didn't know." He turned his scarred face towards Rosa. "I didn't think an innocent soul was to be found in the world anymore. Where on Earth did you find her?"

"It's time we left," said Greg, hauling Rosa to her feet. "Good to see you, men. Hooroo."

A thin man tapped Greg on the shoulder. "Valley, if you have something worthwhile to trade, I have some info for your little chicka here on some water. Upstairs?"

Greg paused for only a heartbeat. "Actually, I have got something to get off my chest." He followed the thin man upstairs and gestured for Rosa to follow. Downstairs had resumed their activity, though too many eyes still followed her and Greg upstairs.

"Thought this was where the bad element hung out?" whispered Rosa.

"It's no different from walking into the Dogs' warehouse, so we'll be fine." He flashed a mischievous smile at her, then resumed his game face. "Best we're careful. We've been dancing too close to the fire lately, and we're bound to get burnt."

Upstairs consisted of two distinct areas. On one side were round tables under clouds of cigar smoke.

Here, people played cards games, and to Rosa's amazement, she saw the glint of coins alongside stacks and stacks of notes.

"Many still play for the old currency in hope of one day being able to use it again," said Greg. "There're many who've left here millionaires—though it won't do them any good."

He indicated the other section with a small nod. A large assortment of tables, some with cards, some dice, some with chips, and some with little figures Rosa couldn't make out sat under the same cloud of smoke. "They're the real games," said Greg. "We're here for the big one, King of the Castle. The buy-ins are the best around. Fingers crossed our little gov secret gets us in."

She peered at the stakes with interest. A pair of steel-toed boots and a small chest sat on one table. A small potted rosebush, a painting of what looked like a building made from tall seashells nested together, and a stack of books lay on another. Rosa walked towards the books, but Greg steered her towards the man waiting to direct them to a game.

"We tell Phil our secret and he matches us with a game of similar stakes," said Greg. "Phil reveals the information to whoever wins."

The man sitting at an empty table at the end of the room seemed to be part of the clouded atmosphere.

"That's Phil," said Greg. "Usher, treasurer, and occasionally dealer extraordinaire."

Phil accepted Greg's whispered buy-in and pointed to the thin man's table.

"This shouldn't take long," said Greg, loud enough for everyone to hear. He leaned down and whispered to Rosa, "I know this game will be riveting, but make sure to watch my back."

Phil circled the table with a velvet rope and ushered Rosa behind it. She tried to catch eyes with Greg but he was staring intently at his opponent. As if the velvet rope were a trigger, people gathered to watch.

Denny touched her arm, and Rosa jumped. She hadn't realised that he'd followed them up. "King of the Castle," he said, "heard of it?"

Rosa shook her head.

"Five cards to make a consecutive run. You need a picture card to play for the Castle, and a king to get the highest score. King means full score, queen half, but a jack counts against you if it's your high card, though not if it's in your run—"

Phil raised his hands for quiet, then promptly dealt the cards. Rosa enjoyed games on the rare occasion of free time, but the games she played at home were quick and fun and loud, not quiet and tense. Greg, however, seemed at ease.

Each man was dealt five cards, then a further three from another deck of Castle cards—property cards from Monopoly. Rosa recognised them from Aire's incomplete set.

A couple of rounds of discarding and further dealing passed until Greg put a small red house in front of him. The crowd murmured. The thin man threw his cards down. Fold.

"They play best of three," said Denny, as the cards were shuffled. "If you put out the little red house, it means you're playing for King of the Castle."

Three-quarters of the pub's patrons now surrounded the table. In the clouded lighting, Rosa struggled to see anyone's faces, let alone a weapon trained on Greg. The thin man won the second round. One all.

The crowd strained at the velvet rope to see the final round, and Rosa found herself almost touching the table. She kept an eye on those within grabbing distance of Greg. A collective intake of breath drew Rosa's attention to the game. Both players had put forward little red houses. Sweat beaded on the thin man's lip. Greg's smile was gone.

Phil called to see the cards. He counted down. "Three. Two."

On one, the cards were thrown down, the crowd surged towards the table, and two shots were fired.

Rosa was pushed to the ground, and someone yelled, "Who shot first?"

Rosa scrambled to her feet. She could see the soles of the thin man's shoes staring at her from under the table. They twitched as people jostled to get a look— or get away. Greg was hurriedly talking to Phil, who passed him a piece of paper. Then Greg's eyes searched for Rosa. He pushed his way to her and walked her down the stairs and out of the pub that was a frenzied anthill. She could feel everyone's eyes follow them out the door, though she didn't look at any faces, afraid of the hostility she might see. As soon as they were outside, she turned to Greg.

"Later," he said. "We have to get out of here."

The door slammed behind them and they both spun around to see Johno rushing to them. "Hang on, I never got to have that word with you. It's not something I want to be a messenger of, but if I never see you again . . . what possessed you to go to the Dogs?"

"You had a word for me?" Greg's tone would have frozen the sun.

Johno nodded. "Right, it's just that, mate, if what I've heard about you is true, if you're a . . ." he hesitated. "No-one knows who any of them are, but if you're one of them, I thought you'd want to know that one of the Dogs who did Joy in is still alive."

The wind blew an eddy of sand past them. Dry leaves caught in it and crackled. Greg's fist clenched, but before Rosa registered why, Johno was on the ground sporting a bloodied nose.

The door of The Well opened and six men piled out, each pulling out knives or metal bars from thin air.

"Start the car," said Greg. "Now."

Rosa didn't need to be told twice. She ran and unlocked the car without fumbling the keys. The six men surrounded Greg. Johno had disappeared.

She jammed the key into the ignition and put a foot inside the car.

"Get in." Greg lifted Rosa bodily and shoved her into the car.

As she sat up, Greg sped off. Rosa stared out the back window. All six men were on the ground.

"That went about as well as we could have hoped," said Greg. "Still copped a gun to the back—two, actually—but that's expected when talking about desal plants. I wish you would have toned down your question a bit so the entire pub didn't hear."

"Really, Greg?" Rosa channelled her fear and frustration into her words. "Maybe you should have told me exactly what to say because apparently, it was worse than shouting, 'I'm going to kill you all.'"

"If you said that, at least everyone would have

laughed. Desal plants are gov territory and government is a bad word at The Well, or anywhere. I did mention this to you when we left Aire. When they tried rationing the water decades ago, the gov put out prop's saying they would build desal plants off the new coastlines all around the country, but that was just a way to get people not to look closely at who was being given the rationed water. I counted on the interest you aroused with your question, but not that the entire pub would think you're a spy. The mercs, the Dogs—if we see any of them again, we'll be stuffed."

"Shouldn't I just have told them I'm a mechanic and I want to try to purify water? That I'm doing it for everyone? Wouldn't that have been easier than your ruse?"

"Oh, Birdie, no. No-one would believe you. I believe you, and I love you for it, but they wouldn't."

"So where are we going? What happened back at The Well?"

"The thin man pulled a gun. He shot at me, and he got shot. That second bullet might have been a bad shot meant for me, too."

"Or someone was trying to save you," said Rosa.

Greg shrugged. He passed her a piece of paper. It took her a moment to work out what she was looking at, but then she gasped aloud. It was a plan to set up a solar desalination process. It used conventional solar panels to desalinate seawater and use it for irrigation.

"Phil told me the location of an old town not too far from here," said Greg. "Supposed to have quality solar panels on every second house. That's where we're headed."

"You never know what the future holds," said Rosa, still eyeing the plans. "The seawater's creeping up on us. My Da used to say that all the time. He was always one step ahead, always trying to ensure Aire's survival. It's not reverse osmosis filters, but I'm sure I can think of something." Rosa reached over and cupped Greg's cheek with her hand. "Thank you, Greg."

"You're all chipper again," he said. "All it took was a new project."

"All it took was your faith in me."

CHAPTER EIGHT: WARDENS

"Remember when I said if we ever saw any of the mercs or Dogs that we'd be stuffed?" said Greg. "Well, we're stuffed."

Rosa looked into the side mirror. A dust storm announced the two cars racing after them.

"I should have known it was a trap," said Greg. "Can't trust anyone in that place."

Greg turned sharply towards a tree line. He drove straight through and emerged amongst blocks of suburban houses. Rosa stared around her in disbelief. She hadn't seen a thing from the road.

Greg floored it, and the Ranger responded, quickly learning his impatience. He zigzagged through the streets of abandoned houses. He drove well, but Rosa didn't think he would be able to shake their pursuers off that easily. He searched the houses they passed, and Rosa realised he wasn't trying to outrun them, he was looking for somewhere to hide.

"Does everyone out here like big cartoon animals?" asked Rosa. A person-sized green dinosaur looked out from one of the abandoned windows.

"What did you see?" asked Greg sharply. "What was it holding and which hand was waving?"

Rosa turned in her seat to watch it pass, a sour feeling bubbling in her stomach. "Left waving, empty-handed."

"Still searching, nothing of interest," said Greg. "Great, that's all we need. If the Dogs have put up the animals, they've taken a breather, but we'd better hope they don't come back while we're here."

Greg turned without warning and drove straight into the lounge of a half-destroyed two-storey house. Rosa covered her head in shock as plaster sheeting crumbled around them. He inched into an adjoining dining room and shut off the engine.

"Follow me," he whispered.

He picked his way through the ruined house until he found the stairs. He climbed, stepping carefully and keeping close to the wall. Rosa followed his footsteps precisely. Halfway, they heard a car slowly driving past. Rosa and Greg stopped, listening. She hoped the house had settled since they had driven through it.

The car idled outside. Greg reached out and grasped Rosa's hand. The minutes ticked by.

Finally, the car drove away.

They finished climbing the stairs. They came to the master bedroom and crept to the front overlooking the street.

"What do you think he is?" said a voice from below them. "Dog or gov?"

Greg grabbed Rosa and held her against the wall.

"Don't reckon it matters," said a second voice. "See the ute he was driving though? It stank of Dog."

Rosa's heart thudded in her ears. She pressed her back into the wall, trying to steady herself. She tried to listen for footsteps coming up the stairs but couldn't hear anything over her heartbeat.

"It's okay, Birdie," said Greg after what felt like an eternity.

She opened her eyes.

"They've gone." Greg took her face into his hands and kissed her. Then he pulled her into his arms. "You know," he said, "it's time I settled down."

Rosa shifted her head so she wouldn't miss a word.

"And I can think of no better place than where you are," he continued. "If that's not in Aire, so be it. I'll follow you, Birdie, wherever you want to go."

The light shining through the broken glass cast rainbows across the floor. Rosa smiled. She kissed Greg's neck, then whispered in his ear, "I'll hold you to that."

"We'll hang around for a little longer to make sure whoever's followed us is gone," he said, smiling, "but if you feel like it, we can take a peek around, see if you find something useful?"

"I'd like that," said Rosa.

They searched the house together, Greg following Rosa's lead. She was finally out salvaging, but she struggled to pay attention. She'd seen the abandoned, broken houses within the rainforest limits, but this was different. After seeing Wonthaggi underwater, she felt the loss of the people who had once lived here more keenly. Greg had only been twelve when his life had been changed forever by the Rise. If he was willing to follow her wherever she went, shouldn't she be willing to do the same for him? Isn't that what love was?

"I'm sorry," said Rosa into the kitchen cupboard she was searching.

Greg was by her side in a flash. "What's this?"

Rosa grinned at his barely contained enthusiasm. "I really mucked up the start of your retirement." She sighed and her face fell. "You're right," she said, "it isn't my world out here. Establishing another settlement would take too long, and people need help now. Seeing what it's like out here . . . I've made up my mind. I have everything I need in Aire. I can devote my life to making life better for others—and, as you said, I shouldn't neglect my family. I'd have to be a mongrel chicken not to see what I have right in front of me. So, Aire first, then who knows? Maybe the world."

Greg chuckled. "Maybe this trip wasn't such a bust after all." Then his face softened. "You're extraordinary, Rosa. You've changed my world. I know you'll change everyone else's."

"If you're in Aire, maybe it won't be so bad," said Rosa. "As long as my workshop stays the same."

"I wouldn't cage you, Birdie," said Greg. "I know you like to be free."

Rosa smiled and flung her arms around him.

She walked over to the section of partially collapsed roof near their car. It was fitted with an array of solar panels. Something turned over in her mind, like a car starting after sitting around for, say, thirty years.

"All the wildlife are mutating in small ways," she said. "The ladybirds, wallabies, even your super octopus. But what they're adapting isn't necessary for their survival. It's like a non-turbo car having a blow-off-valve—it doesn't need the extra pressure release, so why have it at all? It would have to adapt to the extra part for no reason, if that were possible, and then—"

"I agree," he said, "the animals know something we don't. They'll out-survive us all."

Rosa stared at him, unsure if he was teasing her. "The ladybirds and cephalopods are going to gang up on us when we least expect it?" she said, grinning. "You really don't like them, do you? The ladybirds have webbing on their legs, not cannons strapped to their backs."

"It's what you said but brought to its conclusion. They know something we don't."

Rosa shivered.

"How do you know all of this, anyway?" asked Greg.

"It's hard not to notice the webbed claws on a wallaby. Anyway, my Da wanted to make a desalination system for Aire, but we don't need it with the setup we already have. So why was he so passionate about it? Because we should be prepared, like the animals. Exactly what you said. They know the waters are going to keep rising, so the desal plant for Aire, and the technology overall, will be necessary. Lifesaving. You never know what the future holds." She smiled triumphantly.

Greg smiled back at her. "That's what I love

about you, Birdie. Never lose your determination, your desire to do good."

"I'm glad you think so," said Rosa, still beaming. "Look here. There's your stock of solar panels. It might have been a trap, but the directions were right. I won't be returning empty-handed after all. I'll be able to use the panels to create a desal system to use seawater for our hydroponic gardens. We will be prepared."

Greg helped Rosa strap down as many of the panels as possible into the ute's tray.

"Before we drive out of here and find somewhere to kip for the night," said Greg, "I've got something I want to show you." His voice became gruff. "Had it since I last saw my parents. They'd given it to me just before . . ." He trailed off as he reached into his shirt and took out a worn magazine. The pages were thin, and the entire thing looked like it would disintegrate at any moment. Half of the front cover was missing, but it looked like the comic book was about a man who wore yellow and blue, with hair like a wolf's ears.

"I do carry a hero around with me," said Greg. "Just wanted you to know."

***

The road back home looked the same as on the way out,

but to Rosa, it had a hardened edge to it. An inevitability, but also newfound freedom.

The sparse beginnings of her rainforest appeared in the distance. They were almost home.

Greg laughed and tapped the wheel as if he were thinking of the funniest joke. "What a way to go out."

"What do you mean, 'go out?'" asked Rosa. "It's time for you to tell me about everything."

Greg sighed. "No-one knows my secrets. People only suspect or believe rumours that—"

Rosa grabbed the wheel and pulled. Greg's reflexes weren't quick enough to stop the car from veering into a ditch. He slammed on the brakes and they both flew forwards, seat belts digging in painfully.

"What the bloody hell are you doing?" shouted Greg. "We've got enough people trying to kill us without you doing us in, too!"

"I've finally got your attention, have I?" said Rosa, her face hot with anger and pain from her shoulder. "Who is The Valley? What are you? No dodging the question anymore. I need to know who you are, Greg."

Greg put his foot to the floor, sending the ute skidding out of the ditch and showering it with orange clods of dirt and sand. "You want to know who I am? Fine. I'll show you who I am."

They drove in silence for three-quarters of an

hour, parallel to the rainforest. Rosa wasn't sure where Greg was taking her. Had she finally hit his crazy switch? The veins protruding on his arms had not resumed their proper place since she had steered the car off the road.

Then she saw it—a lone black shipping container in the distance. Greg was driving straight for it.

"You want to set a criminal free? Here's your chance."

Greg's voice was so unlike his own that Rosa panicked. She didn't want to see a dead body, but—if they were alive—Rosa *would* release them.

Greg stopped three car lengths from the container. He sat behind the wheel for a long time, staring into the distance. They hadn't yet passed beyond her forest. The container was eerily close to her home, and she had never known about it. When Greg got out, she stepped out too.

Greg came around and hauled her towards the container, though she tried to dig in her heels. He didn't take her to the door though, he took her to the opposite side.

Something was scratched into the paint. Initials. A list of them, and beside them, a tally. Greg stared at them as if he looked at the end of the world.

TR III III I
AF IIIII
LW II
V III III III III III III III
BD IIII

Greg pointed a finger at V. "That's mine."

Rosa's head felt light all of a sudden. She didn't want to hear anymore, but Greg was still talking.

"I'm a Warden, Rosa. *Was* a Warden."

All the reverence, the fear with which others looked at Greg . . . Ridge's question if she knew who Greg really was . . .

"This isn't the only shipping container out here," he said, "but it *is* the one I arranged to be here. So I could be close to you."

Rosa took a few steps back. Then she ran to the car.

Greg caught up with her halfway and pulled her around. "You know who I am now. Is it everything you imagined?"

"I thought you were taking me to free a criminal? Is there . . . is someone inside? Did you put them in there?"

Greg shook his head. "No-one's in there. When someone's enclosed, a sign's put up detailing the crimes they committed. Did you know anyone can set the criminals free, Rosa? Anyone can choose to give them aid—but no-one does. I've been retired for a long time, not that it matters. It was Joy. After Joy, my hunting of criminals changed. It was no longer to serve justice, it was to exact revenge. When I realised what was eating me, what I was doing, I stopped. I haven't put anyone in a container for well over two years. But that's not why I took you here." Greg dropped to his knees, still holding Rosa's hands.

"I did bring you here to set a criminal free," he said. "I deserve to be in that container almost as much as anyone else I ever put there. Put me in the box, Rosa. Set me free from my crimes. If anyone deserves wasteland justice, it's me."

Greg still held her hands, but Rosa was too numb to feel them. "You're right," she said simply. Greg looked up at her. He was shaking a little, and Rosa realised he was sobbing.

She extracted her hands from his grip and wound her fingers through his hair. She paused for a moment. Sunlight was shimmering onto the container, making it both indistinct yet marked. Was this how the heroes felt when they decided the fate of someone they loved?

She fell to her knees and pulled Greg to her. "If I were here to free criminals, why would I condemn you?" Her cheeks were wet with tears. "I do know you, Greg. Whatever you've done, I forgive you."

They grasped one another as if they were dying. Neither would let the other go.

"I love you, Greg."

"I love you, Birdie."

***

Aire was a mass of industry as the residents prepared for Christmas Eve. Clive and the other salvagers had delayed their expedition and were decorating the main common room. No-one was allowed to help Ma Frannie with the cooking. Rosa watched Greg check and reinforce the wooden bridges while she strung fairy lights along the rails.

Since their return, Greg had been busy with his new role as protector, creating a secure and inconspicuous perimeter around Aire, complete with patrols and lookouts. The community had finally listened to Rosa, with assistance from Greg, and though they wouldn't announce anything to the world, Frannie had said she would consider taking in refugees as long as they agreed to stay within Aire's perimeter.

As the sun turned a fiery orange with the day's last light, the residents crowded into the festive common room. Clive had potted a small Mountain Ash and decorated it with salvaged baubles. A small wooden nativity—found on the same salvaging run—was the centrepiece on one of the two long tables laden with food. Dishes of kangaroo meat steaks, sausages and burgers were garnished liberally with rosemary, mint and orange. Fresh leafy greens abounded. Dessert was egg custards flavoured with gum-leaves.

"No-one cooks like you, Ma," said Rosa. She admitted she enjoyed being home . . . a little.

Frannie smiled. "I'm still waiting to hear about you and Greg. Are you going to tell us, or am I going to announce it for you?"

"I don't think it needs an announcement. Everyone already knows I've moved into a larger room with Greg."

"I'll do it, then." Frannie stood with a glass in her hand. "Toast everyone. To my daughter Rosa who we welcome back with open arms."

The residents raised their drinks, some nodding to Rosa.

"And to Greg Valley, our newest member of Aire. We hope they intend to make their partnership official in the near future."

Everyone clapped, even Clive, though he was spending the evening stacking burgers into mountains on his plate. Rosa couldn't help but grin. She looked at Greg who was fiddling with something small and circular in his breast pocket. She was surprised for a moment, then pleased, wondering how he would ask her.

After dinner, most of those with early chores drifted away. Rosa found herself looking out the window of her new tower room. The area was big enough for a family, a gesture of Frannie's that hadn't gone unnoticed by Rosa. She watched the fairy lights twinkling through the trees and enjoyed the fresh scent of mint from her hydroponic garden in the warm night air, her mind full of designs for her solar array.

She adjusted the star atop her small Christmas tree hung with shiny emblems. Before she took her hand away, Greg's fingers cupped hers. She hid her startle by leaning into him. He wore a regular shirt instead of his usual rough utility jacket and he felt soft in comparison. "It's perfect," she said.

Greg smoothed Rosa's hair. "I need you to know, I was always going to tell you about him. I'm not that man anymore. The Valley. What Johno said about Joy when we were leaving The Well—it doesn't matter if there's still someone out there. It doesn't make an ounce of difference because I will not exact revenge anymore. Johno played an underhanded card, and he knew it, which is why he disappeared when those men came out.

If he was trying to rile me into action, it failed."

Greg drew patterns across Rosa's hand with his fingers. "This is perfect. Us. Merry Christmas."

They sat in comfortable silence. The trees whispered to her in the heartening way she had missed on her trip.

Greg looked peaceful, like on that misty morning when he told her he could get used to drinking tea. When he had first told her, she realised, that he would be settling down. With her.

"What are you looking at?" asked Rosa, when he had gazed into her eyes for long moments.

"Diamonds."

Rosa smiled. All would be right with the world, even if it was, for the time being, only their little piece of the world.

ACKNOWLEDGEMENTS

Writing is not a solitary endeavour. Sure, the writer puts pen to paper, but there are so many others that contribute behind the scenes. I would like to take this opportunity to thank those who helped shape River of Diamonds into the story within these pages.

A heartfelt thank you:

To my husband, Tim, for your absolute faith in me. Every time I hesitated, you lifted me up. I cannot find the words to express how much I love you—and for a writer, that's saying something!

To my mother for time, my father for inspiration, and my son for the world.

To my original beta-reader team, Vanessa Mantzaris and Alaine Fraatz, who read my story when it was being created and crafted. Thank you for your time, patience, and enthusiasm. And Alaine, brother, you must have been born with all the patience in the world to continue to read my stories. I am forever grateful.

To Brandi Dixon and Jamie D. Munro. Your editing insights were invaluable. Brandi, your dedication, kindness and all-round amazing ideas brought River of Diamonds home.

To my fellow Drowned Earth authors. It was a

joy going on this adventure with you all.

To Alanah Andrews, for making this all possible. You are extraordinary.

And to God. For everything.

ABOUT THE AUTHOR

S.M. Isaac has always loved books and writing. She circled her calling for years, gaining a BA in literary studies and children's literature, then becoming a qualified automotive parts interpreter which she worked as for eight years before becoming a wife and mother and settling into writing science fiction and fantasy.

She lives on the Surf Coast in Australia with her husband, son, and two cats. She loves reading adventure fantasy, eating sushi, and watching action movies—all at the same time.

https://www.smisaac.com/

ABOUT DEADSET PRESS

Deadset Press is the publishing imprint for Aussie Speculative Fiction – a community aimed at supporting Australian and Kiwi authors. You can learn more at:

www.aussiespeculativefiction.com

ABOUT THE SERIES

Drowned Earth is a series of eight standalone novellas, set in a shared world.

Prequel: Shards of Silver by Alanah Andrews

Debbie is on board a ship when an asteroid collides with Antarctica, causing a tsunami. And it's heading her way… (eBook Only: Free Download)

The Rise by Sue-Ellen Pashley

The great Rise means that resources are scarce and not readily shared. But with her best friend's life at stake, along with some stranded refugees, Katie James knows she must prove there's more to being human than just existing. Even if that puts her on the same kill list.

Fire Over Troubled Water by Nick Marone

Despite winds, torrential rains, storms, and bushfires, a fresh water merchant searches for his lost daughter among the autonomous island communities of flooded eastern New South Wales.

Submerged City by Austin P. Sheehan

Melbourne is under martial law, overseen by general Messinger—an extremist who believes the flood is God's retribution against the left-wing agenda…

Tides of War by Marcus Turner

After discovering a strange man in a row boat, Maria wages war on the lotus cities—clandestine floating communities off the coast of Victoria that are reserved for the wealthy.

The Jindabyne Secret by Jo Hart

With nothing but a map and a rickety solar truck, Jax journeys to the top secret fresh water facility at Lake Jindabyne—one of the few fresh water lakes left in Australia. What he discovers there could be the key to saving his whole community, as long as the government doesn't kill him first.

River of Diamonds by S. M. Isaac

Who would want to leave one of the last idyllic settlements since the Rise? Rosa has a map, a mercenary, and a hope to salvage a future for the world.

Salvaged by C.A. Clark

Cassie lives in the safe haven of academics on the anchored city of new Melbourne. After a diving incident she is rescued by a territorial beach combing gang who trade goods washed up by the frequent storms. Cassie wishes she had never taken her home for granted.

Emoto's Promise by Shel Calopa

Five hundred years after the flood, can Macie defeat the technology which has enslaved the last remaining humans in the walled city of Darwin?

ALSO BY DEADSET PRESS

Annual Anthologies

Beginnings: Australian Speculative Fiction Vol. 1

Journeys: Australian Speculative Fiction Vol. 2

Zodiac Series

Capricorn

Aquarius

Pisces

www.aussiespeculativefiction.com

9 780648 421191